The Big Smith Snatch

The Big Smith Snatch

Jane Louise Curry 11342331

Margaret K. McElderry Books
NEW YORK

Margaret K. McElderry Books
Macmillan Publishing Company
866 Third Avenue,
New York, NY 10022
Collier Macmillan Canada, Inc.
Designed Barbara A. Fitzsimmons

Printed in U.S.A.
First Edition
10   9   8   7   6   5   4   3   2   1
Library of Congress Cataloging-in-Publication Data

Curry, Jane Louise.
The big Smith snatch / Jane Louise Curry.—1st ed.
p.   cm.
Summary: When their pregnant mother gets sick on the eve of their
move from California to Pennsylvania, the four younger Smith
children find themselves in the custody of the city, leaving their
twelve-year-old sister Boo, with the help of eccentric old Auntie
Moss, to somehow trace their whereabouts and get the family back
together again.
[1. Moving, Household—Fiction. 2. Brothers and sisters—Fiction.
3. Old age—Fiction. 4. Family life—Fiction.] I. Title.
PZ7.C936Bh   1989   [Fic]—dc20   89–8036   CIP   AC
ISBN 0–689–50478–0

1

THE SUN WAS SHINING. SCHOOL HAD
been out for three whole weeks. And for lunch
there were cheese sandwiches fancied up with
basil leaves from the garden. It should have been
a great June afternoon in Los Angeles.

It wasn't.

By two o'clock Boo Smith had stuck up only
half of the garage-sale signs. She had a jaggedy
splinter in her thumb. The paper for the signs
was too flimsy-flappy. And the masking tape
didn't want to stick to the rough wood of the
telephone and utility poles. For a moment Boo
felt angry enough to spit nails—but she couldn't
work up to a really good grumble, because as soon
as "spitting nails" popped into her head, the picture that popped in with it made her giggle: herself—short, skinny Belinda Rainbow (horrible,
sticky-cute names!) Smith—marching along Figueroa Street, tacking up garage sale signs like a
two-legged, curly-headed staple gun. Imagining

1

what it would feel like, she could almost taste the sharp metallic tang of the staples. She would have to pucker up her mouth, tuck her tongue into the middle of the pucker, and then . . . *Thwat!-thwat!-thwat!-thwat!*

Actually, staples were exactly what she needed. To fasten up a sign with old, half-dried-out masking tape, she had to wrap the tape all the way around a utility pole or lamppost until it overlapped and stuck to itself. That way one strip at the top of the sign was enough, but even so, telephone poles were fat enough to use up too much tape. The roll was almost finished, and there were still three more signs to go.

The signs themselves were really good. Great, in fact. Sometimes Boo felt embarrassed—like a traitor, but embarrassed—by the wild colors her mother liked, and the nutty designs she painted on every surface within reach—on furniture, cushions and curtains, and even on clothes. But the signs were wonderful. The paper might be too flimsy, but it was yellow and the bright Day-Glo lettering stood out like a shout. The orange of the words *MOVING SALE,* the vivid green *10 to 4, SATURDAY JUNE 28,* and the loud blue *2112 Hobart Street* would hit everyone driving down Figueroa Street smack in the eye. From inside their cars they wouldn't be able to make out the smaller lettering that read *Furniture, Art Work, Children's Clothing, Books, Toys and Household*

Goods—Must Go, or the cartoon Boo's mother had drawn of herself and five goggle-eyed children peering over a huge heap of things for sale. But people coming along the sidewalk could enjoy it, and would know that "Must Go" meant there would be good bargains.

The good bargains were part of the reason, besides running out of tape, that Boo was in a bad mood. Most of the Smith family's furniture was from the Goodwill store, secondhand pieces Mrs. Smith had painted or recovered, and nobody would really miss it. But how could they sell the almost-life-size cardboard cutouts of Clarabelle Cow and Goofy that Mr. Smith had found in a dumpster out behind the video store? Or the picture frames all covered with seashells? Or the croquet set? What if the mallets *were* beat up and half the hoops made from wire clothes hangers? Boo was a good hand with a mallet, and her father said that Grandma's back yard in Pittsburgh, Pennsylvania, was nice and flat. So if they were going to move back there and have a garden that had green grass in summer and not just tomatoes and onions and carrots and squashes, they would *need* a croquet set.

But Boo's mother had said no. Almost everything had to be sold. Elvira—Elvira was the Smiths' elderly Chevrolet van—had to carry Mrs. Smith and Boo and Boo's ten-year-old brother, Cisco, eight-year-old Poppy, and Babba and

Danny, the littlest Smiths, *and* all their belongings from Los Angeles across the desert and mountains and the Mississippi River and Illinois, Indiana, Ohio, and Pennsylvania all the way to Pittsburgh. The Smiths had traveled in Elvira before, so they knew there was exactly enough room in the back for three twin-bed mattresses. Everything else had to fit into the cartons on top of which the mattresses and bedding would rest.

That, alas, meant only one Royal Orchards apple carton for each Smith for clothes and other belongings. There would be five additional cartons for Mr. Smith's tools and the pottery dishes, patchwork quilts, and hand-painted curtains Mrs. Smith had made and for "miscellaneous," and one carton for the Greek myths book and others such as *King Arthur* and *Gulliver's Travels* and the *Canterbury Tales* that the family could not bear to sell, however old and worn they were. The last two boxes would be for food, the first-aid kit, and other items that had to be easy to get at on the trip itself.

It was a sensible plan, Boo knew. And fair. But not *really* fair. How was she supposed to pack her whole life into an apple carton—even a big one? She was three times as old as Danny, the baby of the family, who was only four. So why should Danny have a whole box to himself, with room for all his clothes and Bubba Bear and his wooden train and every one of his favorite things? Why

4

should he, when Boo was going to have to give up the cardboard model of a movie theatre, rows of seats and all, that she had made so that you could look in the front and see your own cartoons roll past on the screen when you turned a crank at the back? And all the big pieces from her collection of rocks? Cisco was lucky. His treasures were tiny: the thirty-odd souvenir pins that decorated his cotton-webbing belt and dotted his favorite T-shirt. It wasn't fair. At all.

Maybe not. Still, Boo supposed she would get over it. She had before, but the last time had been back in second grade when her only real treasures were a family of tiny wooden dolls and a cigar box full of crayons. Six times over the years the Smiths had packed up Elvira and moved. San Francisco to Eureka. Then St. Helena. San Luis Obispo. Santa Ynez. Santa Barbara. They had lived in all sorts of places: in apartments, in Elvira the van, in a trailer, in a motel, and even, once, in a warehouse with five other families. Finally, four years ago, they had come to Los Angeles. To their first-ever honest-to-goodness house. They hadn't been able to afford the rent for one before, because they had been paying the doctors back for Poppy. Poppy, who came third, after Cisco, was born all blue because there was something wrong with her heart and, as Mr. Smith put it, getting it fixed cost an arm and three legs. Each month he paid back a part of what the operation cost, and not until he went to work at Southwest Motors had there been enough left over for the family to rent a real house instead of a just-for-now sort of place.

Boo herself remembered only the moves after San Luis Obispo, but three times was plenty. Half of her hated the thought of another change, but for the other half the prospect of a really green grass lawn in Pittsburgh, and shade trees and her first-ever own bedroom, was delicious. It more than made up for her envy of Susie Loo and Dina Tallman and Nancy Bitts, who would be going on to Nightingale Junior High School without her. Boo didn't know a soul in Pittsburgh—not even Grandma, really, except from postcards and letters—but that part of it she didn't like to think about. Now she concentrated instead on the garage-sale signs and making the tape last.

The next-to-last sign used up all but an inch or two, but it turned out not to matter. Mr. Monahan at Southwest Motors took the last one and put it up in his display-room window with his own tape. Boo's father had been one of his service mechanics until the news from Pittsburgh of Grandma's broken hip and the chance of a job back there changed everything.

"You folks had any word from your dad yet?" Mr. Monahan asked. Mr. Monahan was big and had a bushy mustache and always looked like a walrus whose shirt buttons were going to pop.

6

Boo nodded, edging toward the doorway in case he decided to hug her goodbye. Mr. Monahan might look like a walrus, but he moved more like a big, friendly bear, and he had the kind of hug that could squash a person. She had been squashed once, on her last birthday, and once was enough.

"He phoned," Boo said. But that had been the day after he arrived in Pittsburgh, to say the plane hadn't crashed or anything. Nearly three weeks ago.

"What about the new job? That working out okay?" Mr. Monahan took out his handkerchief to polish a faint fingerprint from the hood of the shiny new convertible by the window.

"I guess so. And we're leaving next Tuesday." *If*, Boo thought. If the postal money order for two hundred dollars out of her father's first paycheck came in time. Without it they wouldn't have enough for all the gasoline Elvira would guzzle.

"Well, I wish your mama luck. Too bad it's not April instead of June," Mr. Monahan said. "I bet you it'll be a long, hot trip. Tell you what. You tell your mama to stop by here on Tuesday and fill up the van's tank at our gas pump out back. You tell her it'll be my going-away present."

Boo headed for home the long way around, by way of the Lucky Food Center. Hurrying on down Figueroa Street, she fell into a daydream

7

about what it would be like to live in the rambling Spanish-style house with the jungly garden far up at the top of Hobart Street. The last of her grumpy mood slipped away. Boo didn't know who lived in the house on the hill, and had no idea what the garden looked like, since she wasn't tall enough to see over the wall, but that only made daydreaming easier. She could imagine a wide, sunny lawn beyond the tangle of trees, and herself setting out hoops for a game of croquet. She would be wearing new white shorts and a floaty, silky pink shirt like the one on the front of a sewing-pattern magazine she had seen at Mrs. Maldonado's next door. She was getting ready for a party. Yes—a going-away party. That was it.

Boo's stride slowed to a dawdle, and the stops and starts of cars at the traffic lights seemed a thousand miles away.

By the time Boo reached the supermarket, her going-away party was already a great success. The striped chocolate-and-vanilla-and-strawberry ice cream in fancy shapes and the fancy party favors were even nicer than the ones at Nancy Bitts's birthday party. Taking a cart, Boo sailed dreamily past the salad dressings, pickles, and chili sauce. Cutting a sharp corner around the end of the row, she narrowly missed an old lady peering at applesauce labels. The old lady gasped and dropped the can she held.

"Oh, I'm sorry. I'm really sorry." Red-faced, Boo scrambled after the can of applesauce as it rolled off down the aisle.

Afterward, at a sedate walk, she headed for the cookies and crackers. Her mother's scribbled list was short: two boxes of saltines, two half-gallons of milk, a giant can of fruit punch, and four boxes of the cheap, "plain-wrap" macaroni-and-cheese dinners. Now, Boo thought, if she were her daydream self, she would probably be shopping for steakburger and tiny baby peas and strawberry cheesecake. But the make-believe had stopped being fun. She was the boring old everyday Boo again.

The walk home wasn't really four miles. It only felt like it. Her kid brother Cisco said it was three quarters of a mile, but things like milk and fruit punch grew heavier by the yard, so that by the halfway point it always felt like four miles. Five, sometimes.

From its bottom end, Hobart Street angled uphill, going straight and easy for a while, but then turning to climb more steeply toward the hilltop. Beyond the turn the houses grew larger, with more trees and shrubbery the farther uphill they sat. The Smith house, half of a shabby old-fashioned duplex, stood three houses below the turn. The seven Smiths lived in the downhill half, Mr. and Mrs. Maldonado (whose children were all grown up and gone) in the uphill half. Even from the bottom of the street it was easy to make out which half of which house was the Smiths' because of the long red-and-yellow-and-purple wind flag that floated out from the TV aerial. No one could miss Elvira, either. She sat in the driveway, a battered old midnight-blue van with faded silver stars and red and gold planets painted here and there all over her.

Fifty yards or so up the sidewalk ahead of her, Boo spotted a familiar thick-set figure in a dark, baggy coat and dirty yellow tennis shoes. Even without the rusty old garden wagon loaded with plastic bags full of belongings that the old woman always pulled along behind her, Boo recognized Auntie Moss. Everyone in the neighborhood knew Auntie.

Mrs. Moss had lived in the Smiths' house before they came. According to Mrs. Maldonado, the old lady had gone half batty after her husband died. Left without enough money to pay the rent and with nowhere to go, she had taken to sleeping in garages and carports when anybody would let her, and in Sycamore Grove Park when they wouldn't. Mrs. Maldonado said she wasn't crazy anymore, but Boo wasn't sure.

Boo didn't like the old woman. Auntie smelled bad, and had sharp, witchy eyes and twisted, knobbly fingers, and sometimes yelled at kids for no reason at all. Even so, Boo was almost glad to see her. Relieved, anyway. No one had seen her for weeks. Everyone had worried vaguely, but nobody had done anything. Mr. Smith's guess was that Auntie had moved downtown to live at the summer campground for homeless people. Cisco thought maybe she'd gone looking for another neighborhood. Either way, Boo supposed she had left because of the way Ronnie Doty and the Kettleman kids always pestered to see what was in the plastic bags heaped up in her wagon, and sang "*Bossy, bossy Flossie Moss! Where's her marbles? Lost, lost, lost!*" in yah-yah voices when she yelled at them to go home and suck green lemons.

Farther up the street, Vern Simmons, the mailman, came trundling his little three-wheeled bag carrier along the Pullers' front walk and onto the sidewalk.

The mail!

Boo broke into a run, the grocery bags swinging and banging against her legs. Vern *had* to have a letter from her father today. The time he telephoned to say he'd gotten to Pittsburgh safely and that Grandma's broken hip was coming along as well as could be expected, he had told her mother to have the telephone disconnected right away so they could save the money. So now even if he wanted to, he couldn't phone to say the money order was on the way. It just was. It had to be, since his first payday was five days ago. And how could a letter take more than five days to come by airplane from Pennsylvania?

11

"Try'na beat that brother of yours to the mail, Rainbow?" Auntie Moss cackled after Boo as she passed.

Boo turned, panting, and trotted backward. "Hi, Mrs. Moss. Where've you been? We've got lots of your mail."

Auntie brightened like a droopy old dog who hears the word *biscuit*. When she smiled, there was a gap where her front teeth should have been. With her cackle and gray, frizzy hair and stoop, all she needed was a hooked nose and pointy chin to look like a fairy-tale witch.

"Real mail?" Auntie asked quickly. "Letters?"

"Maybe. I don't know. I think it's mostly catalogs, that kind of stuff. Where's your wagon?"

"In a safe place," the old woman said craftily. "Where certain nosy brats can't get at it."

"Well . . ." Boo, still walking backward, tried to think of something else to say, but couldn't. "I'll see you up home. I gotta go." She turned and ran.

Vern, the mailman, turned in at the Smiths' front walk before Boo got that far, but she cut across the Winklers' grass next door and got to the mailbox just as he did. Cisco and eight-year-old Poppy came flying out the front door a moment later.

"Is it here?" Cisco sounded as breathless as Boo actually was.

"You kids in some kind of hurry?" Vern sorted

12

slowly through the rubber-banded packets of mail he held. "Here, I guess this batch is yours."

"Thanks, V—" Boo's eye fell on the envelope addressed to *All the Rest of the Smiths* in a familiar scrawl.

"It's here!" She snatched the letter from under the rubber band and, thrusting the rest of the bundle of mail at Cisco, bounded up the porch steps.

"Mom!" Boo banged in through the sagging screen door. *"Mom?* It's here!"

Mrs. Smith was sitting in the middle of the living-room floor with Babba and Danny, the two smallest Smiths, and the five neighborhood children she took care of on weekdays. They were building a castle with the blocks that she had cut out of scrap lumber and painted pink and green and watermelon red when Cisco was little.

Mrs. Smith sat back on her heels looking flushed, but she smiled a broad smile when she saw the envelope Boo waved.

"Thank goodness!" She pushed herself up and crossed to the sofa. "You read it to me, Boo honey."

Boo tore the end off the envelope and unfolded the sheet inside. " 'Dear Ginny, Boo, Cisco, Poppy, Babba, and Danny,' " she read. " 'All is fine here. Grandma is out of the hospital and I rented her a wheelchair so she can move around some on her own. One of the neighbors comes

13

in a couple of times a day to lend a hand, and I'm here at night and morning to carry her up to bed and down again, so we're getting along O.K. without any nurses. The new job is fine too, and I like the people I work with. Buckets of love, Dad.' "

Cisco peered into the envelope, then around the floor. "Mom? Where's the money order?"

2

MRS. SMITH'S HAND FLEW TO HER mouth. "Oh, crumbs! It isn't here. It hasn't come. The envelope. Where's the envelope? What's the date on the postmark?"

Boo snatched the envelope from Cisco. "June nineteen. But that's eight whole days ago!"

"Double crumbs!" Mrs. Smith took a deep breath. "If your Dad couldn't get his paycheck cashed right away last Friday, and if he had to wait till Monday to buy the money order, why . . . if a letter can take eight days, it might not get here till—till after Tuesday."

Boo shut her eyes tight, as if that could shut out both the bad news and her mother's pale, tight, worry look. The look had gone away after Mr. Smith's phone call, but now it was back again, and that was awful. She was going to have a baby—not until September, but worry was bad for you anytime if you were going to have a baby. Boo's friend Mary Lou Kennedy's mother was

15

having one too, and the doctor had told her that. Mrs. Smith couldn't afford to go to a regular doctor, and with Poppy and Babba and Danny and the day-care children to look after all day, she never had time to go sit and wait her turn at the clinic. Boo and Cisco helped out around the house more than before, but she got tired anyway. She always said she wasn't. They didn't trust that.

"It'll come tomorrow," Boo said fiercely. "I know it'll come tomorrow. If it doesn't, we can borrow Mrs. Maldonado's phone and call Daddy collect. He'll figure out what to do."

Cisco handed his mother the rest of the mail, and Boo went to prop the letter on the mantelpiece. She ran her hand over the marbled fireplace and thought how awful it was going to be to leave it, even if Grandma's house back East did have a real one. This one was fake, but she loved it. The mantel shelf was made of real imitation marble, and below it Mrs. Smith had painted in a fireplace opening and marble around it, and even a grate full of logs, right there on the perfectly flat wall. From the front door no one could tell that it wasn't the honest-to-goodness thing.

A heavy step sounded on the front porch, and Mrs. Smith jumped a little where she sat.

"Who ever can that be?"

"Uh-oh! I forgot," Boo hissed. "It's old Mrs. Moss. She's come for her mail. I'll go get it."

16

"Auntie's smelly," Babba announced. "I don't like her."

"You bite your tongue, Miss Barbara Ozma Smith. You'd be smelly too if we didn't have a bathtub," her mother whispered. Then she sighed. "Cisco's already treated me to a cup of tea, but somebody'd better put the kettle back on. Poor old thing—we'll never get rid of her until she's had something."

When Boo returned with the plastic sack full of catalogs, sale notices, invitations to apply for credit cards, and other junk mail that had piled up since the middle of June, Auntie was describing the new camp for the homeless downtown by the Los Angeles River, where she had moved for the summer. Cisco said he thought it would be fun, sleeping outdoors on a cot and taking showers instead of baths. To Boo it sounded dreadful. Standing in line to take a shower, or to use a toilet in a sort of green plastic outdoor cupboard? Hearing strange people coughing and snoring in the dark? And even if you could wash your T-shirts and shorts, how could you iron them? Most mothers didn't bother to iron T-shirts, but Boo's did.

Boo went back to the kitchen, where the kettle was already boiling. After brewing the mug of tea and putting the teabag aside to use again, she stirred in the two spoonfuls of sugar Auntie always wanted, and carried it in to her with a cookie on a saucer.

". . . anyhow, the food's a sight better 'n saltine crackers and sardines for supper," Auntie was saying. "There's meat most times, and cooked vegetables. I know raw's good for you, but cooked sure tastes nice."

She took the mug of tea with a gap-toothed grin of thanks. After a long swallow of tea, she looked around the living room with its bright colors and boxes of battered toys as if she had never seen it before. It must have looked very different when she had lived in it as Mrs. Calvin Moss. As she peered over the rim of her cup at the buttercup-yellow wall, remembering, her eyes grew vague and shiny.

The silence was uncomfortable. Boo wished Auntie would drink up her tea, wrap up her cookie (which she always saved "for later"), and go. Once she was gone, Mrs. Smith could take her afternoon nap. While she slept, Boo and Cisco took the little ones out back. They watched them very carefully because Danny had once started a climbing game, and it had taken almost an hour to coax the frightened climbers down from the top of the big fir tree in the corner of the garden. Usually Boo or Cisco read them Uncle Wiggly stories or led songs like "Itsy-Bitsy Spider" and "Little Rabbit Hopping By" or helped them build castles in the sandbox.

"We're moving," five-year-old Babba announced abruptly. "Our Grandma Smith, back in Pittsburgh in Pennslavania, fell and broked her hip. She needs somebody to take care of her, but nurses cost an awful lot of money. So we're going to go live with her. Daddy says she has this big old house with five whole bedrooms, and he's got a new job in a company that makes cardboard boxes. He fixes their trucks when they break. Our Cousin Jack founded the job for him."

Auntie looked at Babba as if she had just sprouted leaves.

"Soon's our money comes, *we're* going back too. In Elvira." Babba finished. "And we're going to get a new baby."

"In September," Poppy put in.

"Going? Just like that?" Old Auntie shook her head, hard, as if she were having a difficult time making room in it for the new idea.

"Just like that," Cisco said. Cisco was so eager for the trip across the country to start that whenever he thought about it, he bounced up and down as he walked or stood or sat. Sometimes in bed, too.

"Suffering succotash!" Auntie stared at Mrs. Smith. "You mean to say you're driving single-handed across this whole country in that old rattlebucket?" She gave a cackle. "I hope you get there before Christmas. I'd as soon push off for Hawaii in a kitchen strainer as head back East in that old teakettle."

Cisco glared at the old woman. Boo almost

stuck out her tongue. She felt like going to the screen door and holding it open for a heavy hint. Even their mother's smile was a little thin as she reached out for little Danny to settle him on her lap.

"Never you worry. We'll get there. Dan rebuilt Elvira's engine and put in a new radiator just this spring. And he packed us a first-aid box of spare parts."

Auntie, wrapping her cookie in a rumpled piece of paper from one of her deep pockets, gave Mrs. Smith a shrewd look.

"If you ask me, Ginny Smith, you look like you'd fold up before that old van gets you as far as Barstow. Who's gonna drive the rest of the way? Cisco here?"

Mrs. Smith frowned.

"No sense fussing about what can't be helped," she said firmly. "Come Tuesday, we're going. For now, we've got the garage sale all day tomorrow and Sunday afternoon. If everything goes, we ought to make close on a hundred and fifty dollars. The hundred and fifty plus what I've got saved up comes to just about what Dan figured the gas and oil will add up to. And he's sending us some extra from his first paycheck. Even if it doesn't get here before we have to get out of the house, we'll make it. If we stick to peanut-butter-and-jelly sandwiches and aren't on the road more'n a week, we'll make it."

Auntie snorted. "You ever been to a garage sale where everything got sold?" She pushed herself to her feet and gathered up her bag of mail. When she spoke again, it was in an angry growl. "That husband of yours is as dim-witted as a tom turkey. Sending Dorothy and five Munchkins out through the wicked woods in an old tin can on wheels! Pah!"

By late Sunday afternoon the garage sale had made only eighty-seven dollars and eighteen cents. The sofa went for five measly dollars. Nearly half of the furniture was still there, along with five cartons of odds and ends.

"Auntie was right," Mrs. Smith said with a sigh when the last browser had gone. Easing herself down onto the left-over armchair, she pulled a carton close to put her feet on, and took a long swallow from the mug of milky hot tea that Poppy brought from the kitchen. Her eyes and her ankles told how tired she was. She had really pretty ankles, but sometimes, like now, they were swollen up almost as thick as Auntie's.

"I'm *glad* nobody bought my bed," Babba announced.

"That's silly." Cisco looked up from *Otto of the Silver Hand,* which he had found in the going-to-Pittsburgh carton. "The Salvation Army truck's coming tomorrow to take the leftovers."

"All right." Babba nodded her blond head

agreeably. "I'll sell them my bed for twenny dollars." Twenty was as high as Babba could count.

"They don't pay anything, silly. You *give* it to them," Cisco snapped. Seeing Old Paint, the battered, polka-dotted old hobby horse carried out the driveway, its button eyes pleading for rescue, had spoiled the fun of taking in so many dollar bills and quarters and dimes. Cisco had enjoyed counting up the money every hour or so and making little stacks of quarters and dimes, but Old Paint had been his before it was Poppy's or Babba and Danny's, and he was still unhappy. He might be ten, and too old to cry, but his eyes stung when he thought of all the miles faithful Old Paint had carried him. Sold! Somehow it wouldn't have been half so bad just giving it away.

"For free? Then I won't give it to them," Babba said indignantly.

"It's all right, Babba." Mrs. Smith leaned back with her eyes closed. "We'll take your mattress in Elvira instead of Poppy's. Yours is newer anyway."

Babba, satisfied, went out to the front porch where Motorboat, the Maldonados' cat, sat meowing for attention.

"What *will* we do if Daddy's money doesn't get here tomorrow?" Boo asked, forgetting her promise that it was sure to come. How could her mother stay so calm?

Mrs. Smith rubbed the bridge of her nose. Her voice wavered. "I don't know. I know I said we'd go anyhow, but I just don't see how we *can* leave without it. Maybe if I can use the phone next door, I ought to call Mr. Hessell to ask if the new tenants are coming in right away. If they aren't, he might let us stay on for a day or two."

"Or we could take Elvira and camp out where Mrs. Moss is staying," Cisco said hopefully.

"No." His mother straightened, and this time when she spoke her voice was firm. "That camp's for people who don't have anyplace left to go. We've never been that hard up, and now we've got us a home in Pennsylvania. Daddy's money order *is* going to come, and Tuesday morning we're going to head Elvira straight up Figueroa Street to Interstate 70."

"Don't forget Mr. Monahan and the gasoline," Boo reminded her.

"Maybe. We'll see. We sure can use the gas. Maybe we could make him up a sort of thank-you box of some of the stuff out of the garden. We'll have more than we can take with us. Lettuces and spinach, maybe. And some of the onions and baby carrots. We've got loads of those."

But on Monday no letter came.

And the new tenants were to arrive at noon on Tuesday.

Mr. Hessell, the landlord, said he couldn't be sorrier, but that there was absolutely nothing he could do.

Mrs. Maldonado sniffed when she heard that.

23

On Tuesday morning Mr. Maldonado came over with one of his grown-up sons to help load the heavier cartons into the van and fit the mattresses in on top of them. When the new tenants pulled up in front of the house an hour after lunchtime in a big U-Haul truck, Mr. Maldonado made Mrs. Smith move Elvira over into his driveway and come in for a cup of coffee while they all waited for the mailman.

Vern was right on time, but the only mail he brought for the Smiths was their final telephone bill.

Mrs. Smith took a deep breath.

"Good heavens, the way you kids look, you'd think it was the end of the world. It isn't any such thing." She put her arms around Boo and gave her a sharp hug. "And you, Cisco! No need to look like somebody busted your balloon. We'll just take off anyway."

"Hurrah!" yelled Poppy, who was tiny for eight, bright, big-eyed and pigtailed, and usually the quietest of all.

"No, no, Ginny! How can you?" Mrs. Maldonado threw up her hands. "You won't have enough money for the gasoline. Or for an emergency. What if one of the little ones should fall ill!"

The children could tell from their mother's tight-cornered smile that her mind was made up.

"We'll be stopping a couple of nights in Texas. My brother lives in Wichita Falls," she said. "He can lend us some more if we need it."

24

Mr. and Mrs. Maldonado tried to talk Mrs. Smith into staying at least until the next morning. She and the children could have dinner with the Maldonados and use their little downstairs bathroom and spend the night in Elvira right there in the driveway.

Mrs. Smith wasn't to be budged. "No. It's not that we don't appreciate the offer. Honestly, we do."

She drew another deep breath. "It's just I've got this now-or-never feeling. Tomorrow morning we'd say 'Wait till Vern comes with the mail,' and if the letter doesn't get here there'd be another day shot and we'd probably talk ourselves into staying over again. If we take off now, we can beat the traffic and maybe make it to Barstow before dark. Victorville, anyhow."

The children knew from Mr. Maldonado's frown that he didn't approve. But he, too, knew how stubborn Mrs. Smith was in her quiet way.

"Where will you stay? Campgrounds cost money."

Mrs. Smith's smile relaxed a little. "Oh, Dan figured that out the first time we ever moved."

"I know!" Boo giggled as she remembered. "You make sure the van's all tidy inside and the kids all cleaned up and quiet as angels. Then you drive up to the police station just before dark, and Mom and Daddy take the baby in and ask where's a safe place to park."

Mrs. Smith nodded. "That's right. They'd take

25

one look at the baby and Boo's big brown eyes and figure something out—a church parking lot maybe, sometimes even a motel lot if there was a soft-hearted manager. We ended up out back of police stations more than once."

"*Ay, Dios!*" Mrs. Maldonado threw up her hands again. "I give up."

Elvira didn't make it as far as Victorville.

Elvira didn't even make it as far as Southwest Motors.

At the bottom of Hobart Street, Mrs. Smith turned the corner and pulled up at the curb.

"What's the matter?" Cisco, sitting in the front passenger seat, leaned across to peer at the dashboard. The gasoline was down to half, but the readings on the oil and temperature looked fine.

"What did we forget?" Boo asked from the back.

"Nothing."

Mrs. Smith rested her crossed arms atop the steering wheel and leaned forward to pillow her forehead on them.

"It's just a headache," she said in a muffled voice. "From the excitement. I figured it would go away soon as the suspense was over, but I can hardly see to drive straight."

"You mean we *can't* go?" Boo's insides felt as if someone had squeezed them like a dish sponge.

Poppy was the practical one. "We can go back

up to the Maldonados' driveway. We'll go play somewhere and you can take a nap. It'll be better to leave tomorrow morning anyhow."

Mrs. Smith shook her head without lifting it from the steering wheel. "No. The Maldonados weren't going to say anything about it, but I know their son Rudy and his family are due in from Vallejo tonight. Thirteen people lining up to brush their teeth is a good six too many."

"But they've got two bathrooms," Boo protested anxiously.

"I know, Boo. But we'd just be in the way, and I'd have everybody fussing over me. I couldn't take that. All I need is a good, long sleep somewheres."

Cisco sat up straight. "You mean where Auntie goes?"

"Oh, no!" Boo wailed. "We don't *belong* where she goes. I'll *die* if we have to go there. It's—it's like a city dump, only for people instead of garbage."

She bit her lip, but too late. The words were already out.

Mrs. Smith lifted her head in heavy-eyed dismay. "Oh, Boo! You sound like that horrible stuck-up Mr. Potter who used to live across the street. The one you called 'Old Snooty.' " She drew a long breath. "Boo, I can't argue with you now. Everybody just shut up for five minutes and let me breathe."

* * *

Ten minutes later, Elvira moved on cautiously, heading toward Figueroa Street, Pasadena Avenue, downtown, and the sun-baked camp on the east bank of the Los Angeles River.

3

BOO CRADLED THE PRECIOUS PLASTIC
grocery bag on her knees as she sat on the edge
of the bus seat. The bag was precious because of
the envelope tucked inside the magazine at its
bottom, not because of the bread and milk on
top. Mr. Smith's letter had come that morning.
Wednesday. With the postal money order. The
long bus ride on a hot day with transfers going
and coming and the walk to the Maldonados'
house had been worth every sticky moment.

The letter was addressed to Mrs. Virginia
Smith, but Boo had opened it to make sure the
money order was really there. Her mother, knowing how hard waiting would be, had given her
permission. Mrs. Smith had spent an uncomfortable night in Elvira with the children and was
still feeling tired and headachy. She had decided
to stay put and rest so that she could be sure of
feeling well for an early start on Thursday
morning.

The money order was beautiful. The amount was spelled out in letters as well as numbers—*$200.00 TWO HUNDRED DOLLARS*—so that there could be no mistake. It also said DO NOT FOLD, so Boo had tucked it and the letter into the copy of the *Reader's Digest* Mrs. Maldonado gave her for her mother. A money order couldn't blow out of an envelope at the bottom of a grocery bag, but Boo felt better having it disguised, not just hidden. To be safer still, she had tied the bag's plastic handles in a tight knot.

Boo pushed the bus's buzzer button for the first stop on the far side of the bridge across the river channel. As she stepped down onto the pavement—there was no sidewalk—the door closed behind her with a low *whoosh-whoomp* and the bus pulled away, leaving her alone on the street, feeling like a castaway on an unfriendly coast. Several cars rushed by, but the street outside the campground fence had a deserted air. The warehouses across Seventh Street had a bleak, blank-faced look that even in the late-afternoon sunshine was spooky.

Boo hated the high chain-link fence around the campground. And she hated the camp gate with its guard even if the guards *were* friendly and didn't make you feel like a cockroach. Still, because of the spookiness it felt a lot safer being inside the fence than out. The Salvation Army officers on duty searched all grownups as they came in, to be sure that they stuck to the rules about no knives or guns or drugs or liquor. And a fence down the middle of the camp divided the canopies-and-cots side from the tents side. The men who didn't have families slept on canvas army cots under canopies with pretty scalloped edges that looked as if they had been made to shade fancy picnic parties. Most of the married couples, and the many families with children, and the women all on their own, lived in bubble tents scattered in clusters down the dusty, open space that had until recently been full of old warehouses. Boo hated it all, from the dust to the laundry hanging any old way on the chain-link fence to all the glum faces that stood in line for the free dinner.

But all that was over. Everything was different. Now that the money order had come, the awfulness didn't matter. Tomorrow morning—*early* tomorrow morning—Elvira would roll out through the gate and off to Pennsylvania. Boo couldn't wait to give the news to her mother and Cisco and Poppy and the little ones. But then, it did feel delicious to be the only one who knew. Like being a fairy godmother with a two-hundred-dollar wand.

Boo slipped in through the gate while the guard was trying to explain to a newcomer about registering and where to go to do it. She was so full of her good news and the thought that she was only days—seven or eight at the most—away from having a bedroom all to herself, that she was nearly past the white TV-news station wagon parked several yards inside the gate before she saw what it was. CHANNEL 7 EYEWITNESS NEWS, the sign on its side announced.

The cameraman was at the station wagon's open rear door, packing his video camera into a shiny metal case. The door on the driver's side was open too, and a woman sat sideways on the seat, writing on a notepad. Alarmed, Boo walked quickly past. She kept her head down. What if the man suddenly decided he needed more pictures and pointed the camera her way? Oh, please, *no,* she wished fiercely. It would be awful. Worse than having a monster earthquake hit and open up a crack in the ground to swallow her.

Much worse. Because she might end up on the six-o'clock news.

It was a horrible thought. Susie or Dina or Nancy or her whole *class* might see her! So what if she might never be going to see them again? If it did happen, she absolutely *couldn't* ever see them again. She would shrivel up and die.

Boo slowed down, afraid that hurrying might make the TV man notice her, and she had gone only a few yards when an even more dreadful thought stabbed her. What if the TV people had already photographed and interviewed her mother? Or the kids? Mrs. Smith was so nice she would talk to anybody. And Cisco, if he was asked, would probably make the camp sound like a Great Adventure. Worst of all, Babba (Cisco called her Blabba) would blab all sorts of private, family things to anyone who would listen. She had such curly blond hair and long eyelashes and greeny-blue eyes that everyone always listened like mad, and said "Isn't she adorable!" Anything she said on camera would probably end up showing all across the country on some network news story about homeless people. Everyone in the whole state of Pennsylvania would see it. If any of the students or teachers at Boo's new school ever saw Babba or Mrs. Smith, who was small, and had dark hair like Boo's, they would recognize them and remember. They would remember the camp and the mattresses crowded into Elvira, and all of it. Even if only one remembered, everyone would hear about it. "Didn't I see your family on TV last summer?" they would ask. "Weren't you all at that camp in California where the grungy street people and weird old bag ladies live?" The news would buzz all over school before she had a chance to turn the camp into a funny story or a Cisco-style adventure.

Boo's eyes smarted, but she was too angry to cry. She kicked at the ground instead and raised a small cloud of dust.

"Belinda!"

Startled to hear a man's voice call her by the

name no one ever used—except her parents when she had done something she shouldn't— Boo looked up. Halfway down the block-long enclosure, a man waved at her from under a canopy rigged with a blanket between the open trunk lid of a car and two flimsy poles. The man was Mr.— Atkinson? Allison? Allison. Mrs. Allison took the bus to work every morning at a quarter past six, and Mr. Allison sat all day in an old aluminum beach chair, guarding their car full of belongings and waiting for his broken leg to mend. He kept it stretched out, with the cast propped up on an empty peach crate. The Allisons' old green Pontiac had been parked next to Elvira.

Had been.

Elvira was gone.

Boo stopped dead, frozen in fright. What had happened? Why—*where* had they gone without her?

"Hey, there! Belinda Smith!" Mr. Allison called and beckoned again.

"Where's our van? Where'd they go?" Boo shrieked, the TV news camera forgotten. She broke into a run and was halfway to the Allisons' car before she saw that Mr. Allison was not waving wildly, but flapping his hands at her to stop and then pointing.

"Oi! Over there, Belinda. Out on the street," Mr. Allison called. He pointed back the way Boo had come.

It was a moment before Boo spotted Elvira

through the chain-link fence. The van sat halfway down the first little side street between the warehouses to the north, across Seventh Street. A hand waved from the driver's window. Boo, in relief, waved wildly and ran back toward the gate.

Of course! Her mother was keeping clear of the television news people too. She wouldn't want to take a chance that Mr. Smith in Pennsylvania might catch sight of them on TV. All he would know was that something awful had gone wrong and, not knowing what, he would be terribly frightened. Boo felt a pang of guilt as she raced, grocery bag swinging, across the hot, sandy ground. She had tied herself in granny knots over what might happen at school in September and hadn't given a thought to her father. Or Grandma.

It was a relief, for everyone's sake, to see the Eyewitness News station wagon vanishing up Seventh Street as she hurried out through the gate.

The sun was too hot for running far. Turning onto Seventh Street, Boo trotted slowly along the camp fence for a few yards, waiting for a gap in the traffic. There was no crosswalk. When her chance came, she raced for the other side. Elvira moved slowly to meet her—slowly and jerkily, with a brief, alarming sound of grinding gears. The van stalled with an abrupt hiccup and shudder as Boo came alongside. The passenger door opened.

Auntie Moss sat in the driver's seat.

And she was alone.

"What are you doing in our van?" Boo backed away. Her voice rose. "Where's my mom? Where are the kids?"

"No need to screech!" Auntie's knobbly hands batted nervously around the steering column in search of the ignition key, to turn it off. "Stupid manual gear shifts. I can't stand 'em."

Boo was furious. Scrambling in on the passenger side, she reached across to snatch the keys from the ignition switch. Slipping back down from the seat to stand defiant in the street, she jammed the key ring in her jeans pocket.

"You tell me where my mom is," she demanded loudly. "This minute. Or I'll go across and get the gate guard to call the cops. I'll tell him you stole our van."

"Keep your hair on, you horrible child," the old lady snapped. "Who'd want to steal this four-wheeled disaster zone? And aren't I *trying* to tell you? Why d'you think I asked that Mr. Allison to let you know I was out here? Your mom's in the hospital, that's why. She's in the hospital and half an hour ago one of those busybody social workers came and carted your brats off to the kiddie bin."

A miserable Boo sat at the table by the front window of Frank's Coffee Spot while Auntie Moss waited at the counter. The little lunch bar was well named: the tabletop was covered with coffee spots and rings, and traces of ketchup and something greasy. Boo sat with her hands in her lap.

Auntie had explained everything while she drove Elvira down Spring Street and up Main looking for a parking place and a pay phone. They had found a space with half an hour left on the parking meter, and Auntie had led the way into Frank's. Boo, frightened by what she had heard, had followed without an argument. Her mom in the hospital? The kids probably shut up in a place called MacLaren Hall? It was all so unexpected, so scary, that she felt she was in a story happening to someone else.

Word had gone around before Boo left the campground in midmorning on her expedition to the Maldonados' house that a nurse was coming to take a look at anyone who needed first aid. Because none of the Smiths had cuts or scratches or bumps or bruises, Boo had paid no attention. But according to Auntie Moss, just before noon Boo's mother had gone for a bucket of water and begun to wash out a pair of jeans. Danny had used them for sitting down in the muddy patch under a water faucet. In the middle of wringing out the jeans, Mrs. Smith had keeled over in a dead faint. Auntie (to hear Auntie tell it) ran for the visiting nurse and dragged her back to the Smiths' van. The nurse and one of the tent people nearby helped Mrs. Smith into the shade of the Allisons' canopy as soon as she came around. But

37

the nurse, after that first look, didn't stop to check Mrs. Smith's pulse or her temperature. Instead, ordering her to lie still, she ran to the office trailer to tell the camp director to call not the paramedics but a doctor. The doctor, when he finally came, took Mrs. Smith's blood pressure, asked a lot of questions, and frowned at every answer. He said, Auntie reported, that it looked like "EPH-something." Whatever EPH-whatever-it-was was. Then he gave Boo's mother a shot and sent the nurse back to the office trailer to call for an ambulance. The Salvation Army officer who came over to investigate went off to call the county's Children's Services office to ask them to send someone to take charge of the children.

At that, Boo's mother had protested that she was not going, would not go, could not go to the hospital, and no social worker was taking charge of her children. But before long the shot the doctor had given her made her too sleepy to argue. By the time the ambulance came she was fast asleep, even with Babba howling in fright and Danny shrieking like a teakettle. Poppy was as pasty-pale as mashed potatoes, and Cisco kept saying over and over again in a tight, squeaky voice, "It'll be okay. Boo'll call Daddy and he'll know what to do. It'll be okay." When the ambulance had gone, he and Poppy made peanut-butter-and-jelly sandwiches. The sandwiches finally shut the little ones up.

38

Auntie by then had headed for her own tent and the wagon full of belongings over which her next-tent neighbor was keeping a lookout. Rule number one in Auntie's book was "steer clear of social workers and do-gooders." She didn't like anyone telling her what to do or trying to get her to sign papers, and so she meant to lie low. Instead, she found herself dragging her bubble tent over to stand near Elvira and wheeling her wagon across to park beside it. Not because of the children. "Can't stand kids. Any kids," she had growled to Boo. But because she liked Mrs. Smith and remembered her many past kindnesses, the least she felt she could do was to stand guard over the van. If it landed in the police vehicle pound there would probably be forms to fill out in triplicate and a nasty fine to pay. It might take days to ransom it.

In the middle of the afternoon a woman had turned up to collect the children. She showed Mrs. Moss a card that identified her as a case worker from the Children's Services office and explained that since the children's mother was going to be in the hospital for a while, and since Mrs. Moss, their auntie, was too old to cope with four young children, the city would have to take them "into care." Boo cringed at the thought that anyone could take Mrs. Moss to be "their auntie" and only half heard her go on to explain that "into care" meant they would be farmed out to temporary foster homes or stuck into MacLaren Hall, the juvenile detention center. Auntie's answer, Boo gathered, had been "Okay by me."

"Four. You said four. Didn't she know about me?" Boo asked as Auntie brought a tall cup of grape soda, an extra plastic cup, and two small powdered doughnuts to the table by the window.

"Not from me." Auntie poured soda from one cup into the other, with a sharp eye to keeping the level even in the two. She pushed one toward Boo. "Or from that Cisco of yours. I told him, 'Keep your trap shut, and don't ever answer questions nobody asks.' I figure you can get hold of your dad a lot faster on your own, without getting wrapped up to the eyebrows in their rules and red tape." She gave a snort. "Some of 'em even *talk* like two-legged file cabinets. Wouldn't surprise me if they have to fill out forms in triplicate when they want to go to the bathroom." She dipped a doughnut in her grape soda and took a large bite.

Boo couldn't help the giggle that rose like a bubble through her anxiety. But even if Auntie was a little bit crazy, she was probably right about the phone call.

"If we don't know what's really wrong with Mom or where the kids are, what do I tell Daddy?"

"What in blazes is that stuff you keep between

40

your ears? Oatmeal?" Old Mrs. Moss brushed doughnut crumbs onto the floor with an impatient sweep of her sleeve. "What do you *know* to tell him? Tell him your mom's at County-USC Medical Center and the Children's Services has you kiddies, and the van's at the campground with me. The rest he can find out better'n you can."

She pointed. "Go call. The pay phone's on the wall over there, and back in Pennsylvania it's already past suppertime. You put in a couple of dimes, call collect, and be sure the phone gives your dimes back."

There was only one problem. "I can't." Boo tried to keep her voice from trembling. "I don't know the number."

The old woman glared. "You're a fat lot of help. Probably couldn't find your way out of a soggy paper bag if you had a map." She sat growling to herself for a moment, and then shrugged. "Okay. What you do is call Information. All you need's the name and address. They look up your Granny's number, you write it down, and then you call. That too hard for you?"

Boo blushed. "No," she said stiffly. "Except . . . I don't exactly remember Grandma's address."

Auntie Moss sniffed. "Some grandkid you are," she said sourly. "Don't you ever write letters to your granny?"

Boo forgot about wanting to cry, and snapped, "I do too! Only my letters always go in the envelopes Daddy addresses for his." As she spoke, she remembered the return address on the envelope hidden at the bottom of her grocery bag, and hurriedly unknotted its handles. From Auntie's expression she could see another nasty crack coming, so she stood, fished in her pocket for the coins left over from her bus fare, and stalked to the telephone. Auntie didn't know about the money order, and she didn't need to know now.

Unfortunately the envelope, addressed in Mr. Smith's swoopy scrawl, was not much help. The house number in the upper left-hand corner was 519, but Boo could not make out the name. It looked a little like Willett—at least it seemed to have two Ls in the middle—but it might just as easily have been Millett or Mullard. Or Bullock. She stuffed the envelope back between the pages of the *Reader's Digest* and turned to the phone book. In the front were directions for long-distance directory assistance, and on another page a list of area codes in other parts of the country. Boo dropped two dimes in the slot and pushed the buttons for (412) 555-1212 for Pittsburgh, Pennsylvania. The dimes came back, just as Auntie said they would.

"Fifty cents, please." The voice was a recording. Boo made a face and counted her money.

42

Seventy-eight cents. Period. Grudgingly, she dropped a quarter, the two dimes, and a nickel in the slot.

All for nothing, as it turned out. According to the operator in Pennsylvania, there was no listing in Pittsburgh for an Alice Smith or Alice Mary Smith or A. M. Smith, or even A. Smith. And no Smiths were listed for Willett or Willard or Millet or Mullard Streets. Or Ballard or Bullock. The operator must have heard the panic in Boo's voice, because suddenly she said, "Don't hang up, honey. Think. Is there some other name the residence could be listed under? A husband? A parent?"

"No, thank you," Boo said, and hung up quickly. How could she say to a perfect stranger that it must still be under her grandfather's name but she didn't know what his name *was*? Grandpa Smith had died before she was born; she had never even seen a picture of him, and wasn't sure she had ever heard his first name in the first place. She certainly wasn't going to say so with Auntie sitting within earshot and already thinking she was about as intelligent as a head of lettuce.

For a moment Boo stared at the wall, thinking fiercely, then stiffened. An idea so simple and Ciscoish had popped into her head that she knew there had to be a snag in it. For a moment she was almost afraid to breathe. She dropped her last twenty-eight cents back in her pocket one coin at a time and then, almost without deciding to, headed for the door.

"Come on," she said as she passed Auntie at the window table. "We're going back to the campground. You have to take a shower."

Auntie stared after her, then scraped her chair back and heaved herself to her feet. When she pushed out through the plastic-strip curtain that shaded the Coffee Spot doorway, Boo was already halfway down the block toward Elvira's parking space.

The old woman was panting when she caught up, and red-faced with anger. "Who in Timbuctoo do you think you are, you mean-mouthed little midget, to tell me I gotta take a shower?"

Hurriedly, Boo unlocked Elvira's passenger door and, pretending she had dropped something, leaned over to grope under the seat. Her mother always carried the grocery-shopping money and her driver's license in her little shoulder bag, but the big patchwork bag—and the old blue plastic pencil case where she kept important papers and any other money—always went under the seat. It was still there. Relieved, Boo climbed in, and leaned over to open the driver's door without answering Auntie's angry question. The old woman stomped into the street, looked both ways suspiciously, then hoisted herself into the driver's seat. Boo handed the keys over and crossed her arms on her chest as if to say, "Well, what are you waiting for?" but still said nothing. She was too busy thinking. Auntie fixed her with a sharp, mistrustful look, squinting her eyes up, and then cackled.

"Something's going on in that coconut of yours. How's come I'm supposed to take this shower?"

"Because," Boo said, "we're going to the hospital to see how Mom is and find out if the hospital has called Daddy. Even if they have, I'll get Grandma's phone number from Mom." She drew a deep breath. "And if you go like that, I bet they won't even let us in the front door."

Auntie blinked. Then her eyes narrowed. "Like what?"

"Like—like—" Boo wanted to say "Like a cross between a scarecrow and a laundry basket full of smelly old socks," but she didn't dare make Auntie any madder. She needed her.

"Like *that*," she evaded, and plunged on. "And afterward we'll find out where the kids are and get them back."

"Get them back?" Elvira bucked violently as Auntie accidentally stepped on the gas and the brake at the same time. "What in blazes for? I just got rid of the little noisebuckets."

"If Mom said no social worker could take her kids, that's what she meant." Boo felt less miserable but more nervous now that she had made up her mind. "We've got to be together and ready to go as soon as she's out. Besides, if they farmed us out like you said, Danny'd scream himself silly and Poppy'd worry herself into being sick." Babba, of course, would do fine just about anywhere, the way people fell all over themselves about her curls and blue eyes. But Cisco, though he would never let on, would be scared spitless. So she had to do something. She certainly wasn't going to walk in and give herself up. Or hide out by herself in Elvira, either.

Auntie gave one of her nasty Wicked Witch of the West cackles. "And what'll you do, Miss Prissy? Waltz in to the Children's Services offices and say, 'Hand over the Smith kids, pretty please'?"

"No." Boo looked straight ahead up Main Street. "But you can."

She held her breath.

"*Me?*" Both Auntie and the van swerved and then recovered. "Not on your Nelly! Keep your nose out of hornets' nests: that's my rule. I don't want those busybodies buzzing around me, telling me 'Do-this-do-that-eat-this-stay-here-go-there.' Telling them to buzz off doesn't do a bit of good. They just shake their heads that way that means 'We know best, dearie.' Besides"—her voice took on a sarcastic edge—"what's it all got to do with dirty, crazy old Auntie Moss?"

Boo's cheeks reddened. "I didn't—don't mean it that way. Not really," she protested. Somehow the protest started as a lie, but came out true. "You've *got* to come," she pleaded.

46

Something in the way she said it made Auntie give her a look that was sharp, puzzled, and suspicious all at once.

"Give me a good reason."

Boo took a deep breath and wished Cisco weren't off being a prisoner somewhere. He was a lot better than she was at weaving plots.

"You're going to be our aunt," she said. "For real."

4

CISCO WONDERED HOW BABBA DID IT. Here they were, prisoners, snatched away from home—away from Elvira, anyway—by the awful Ms. Cooperman and lined up in a row on an office sofa ready for interrogation, and what did Babba do? Did she sit up straight and look brave, so that they could be the four fearless Smiths standing (well, sitting) shoulder to shoulder against the dreaded Dragon Lady? Not old Babba. Babba stuck her thumb in her mouth, curled up on the stiff cushion, and dropped off to sleep.

She was really sleeping, too, not playing possum like Danny. Danny might be the baby, but *he* had sense enough to be scared. He sat with his back against the cushioned sofa back, his chubby legs sticking straight out. His blond head lolled forward, but Cisco, sneaking a look at him sideways, could see his eyes flicker here and there around the office as if he were a mouse scouting out a handy hole to use in case of an emergency.

Poppy looked as scared as Cisco felt. Her freckled skin was paler than ever against the dark hair she wore pulled back and plaited into long braids, and she sat up straight and stiff. And trembly. Cisco was half afraid to touch her for fear she might shoot across the room, *twang-g-g!*, like a rubber band when it breaks. Poppy, Cisco decided, was about the bravest person he knew. She was scared of everything, but never ran away or even hid her eyes.

Ms. Cooperman, whose office it was, didn't look much like a Dragon Lady. It was just that except for witches Cisco couldn't think of any other kind of female villain. There were lady vampires, of course. But they didn't bother to kidnap you. They just drank your blood wherever they caught you. A Dragon Lady, once she trapped you, might lock you up and hold you for ransom. The real kind, Cisco knew from watching a lot of old movies on TV, had long, shiny black hair pulled back into fat, shiny black knobs or twists at the napes of their necks, and wore dangly earrings and high-necked slinky dresses and could order you to be dropped into a pit full of snakes or crocodiles at the drop of a hat. Ms. Cooperman looked fierce, but fierce like somebody's mother at five-thirty in the afternoon who had until six o'clock to clean the house, weed the garden, give the dog a bath, and cook dinner. She did wear dangly earrings, but her frizzy-curly brown hair was too short to pull back, and instead of a slinky dress she wore a baggy tan shirt belted over a tan skirt.

Still, you couldn't trust the ordinary hair or ordinary clothes or Ms. Cooperman's frazzled end-of-the-day look. The office was full of warning clues. The books on her bookshelves were arranged by size, and were all exactly in line. Her magazines were filed on their own shelves in their own special boxes neatly labeled with titles and dates. And the five tidy stacks of file folders on the desk were lined up in a row so straight that Cisco decided she must have drawn a guideline on the desktop. It was obvious: the somebody's-mother look was only a fiendishly clever disguise. If Ms. Cooperman couldn't tidy you into line, Cisco decided, she would cheerfully drop you into whatever she had instead of a crocodile pit.

"Now, let's see what to do about the four of you." Ms. Cooperman's strained smile looked pasted on. "I'm sure you're unhappy about being here. And I know you would like to be able to visit your mother to be sure she's all right. But that will have to wait. I called the hospital, and they say she's having a good sleep, and has to have lots more before she can start to get better. So you'll be staying with us for a little while, but only until we can find somewhere better. Perhaps with relatives, or in a nice foster home."

Foster home! For a moment Cisco's mouth

went so dry he couldn't even croak out "No!" But then he calmed down. The Dragon Lady only thought she had the right to say where the Smiths were going to stay. She didn't. As soon as Boo phoned their father, he would phone Ms. Cooperman and say, "I've fixed it up for my kids to stay at Mr. and Mrs. Maldonado's house tonight." Or maybe even "Put my kids on the next airplane for Pittsburgh, Pennsylvania." Until then maybe it was safer not to argue.

"So." Ms. Cooperman rolled a printed form into her electric typewriter, lined up the first blank, and typed a short blur of letters. "I have some easy questions for you. We have your mother's name, Virginia Smith, and her temporary address at the urban campground. And I need to know your names. Oldest first, please." She looked at Cisco.

"Cisco."

"Cisco?" Ms. Cooperman blinked. "No, not your nickname, dear. Your whole real name."

Cisco could feel his cheeks grow red. He ducked his head and mumbled, "San Francisco Moonlight Smith." The Francisco part was okay, but the first thing he was going to do when he grew up was go to court and get a judge to take away the San and the Moonlight. Even his mother admitted that, though she had thought it beautiful when he was a baby, it sounded a little goofy now.

51

"San Francisco Moonlight Smith," Ms. Cooperman muttered. Her fingers flew over the typewriter keys. "And what's your name, dear?" She looked at Poppy.

Poppy's whisper was so small that not even Cisco could hear it.

"What was that, dear?"

Poppy was too frightened to answer, so Cisco spoke up for her. "She's Poppy Luisa Smith. And that's Babba. She's Barbara Ozma Smith. And Danny. His middle name's Christmas."

Cisco remembered Auntie's advice about not answering questions that nobody had asked. It was *hard* not to. He would have liked to explain that his mother liked names that reminded her of something special about every baby's arrival. Danny's middle name had almost been Freeway because he was almost born on the way to the hospital instead of in it. But Mr. Smith and Boo and Cisco had voted against Freeway, so Mrs. Smith settled for Christmas. That was what day it was. The day Boo was born, there had been a beautiful big rainbow—the name Belinda meant "beautiful"—right over the hospital. A big, yellow moon shone over San Francisco Bay the night Cisco arrived. "Poppy Luisa" stood for the hillside covered with springtime poppies that the Smiths could see from their front door the year they lived outside of San Luis Obispo. In Santa Barbara Mrs. Smith had been reading *The Wizard of Oz* to

Boo and Cisco right up to the time to go to the hospital, and that was why Babba ended up Barbara Ozma. It was a pretty nutty way to pick names, Cisco thought. Every once in a while it felt really good to have a name nobody else in the world had. Mostly it was just embarrassing.

Ms. Cooperman didn't crack a smile at the names. That surprised Cisco. Everyone else grinned, or tried hard not to, or thought you were pulling their legs. Ms. Cooperman didn't even raise her eyebrows as she repeated the names under her breath and typed away in short, fast bursts. But then the Dragon Ladies in old movies always were cool and calm in a spooky sort of way. You could never guess what they were thinking. Or when they were going to stiffen up and breathe fire at you. So to speak. He held his breath.

"Right." Ms. Cooperman's finger hovered over the keys. "Now, I need to know your ages, and what schools you and Poppy went to this past year, Francisco. For the rest of the family information I can get in touch with your aunt—your great-aunt? How old are you?"

Cisco didn't answer. From old prisoner-of-war movies he knew that the prisoners didn't have to tell anything but their names, ranks, and serial numbers, whatever serial numbers were. Cisco considered making up a rank, something like Deputy Head-of-Family, and a number, but decided that would sound like a joke. Or little-kid make-believe. The pickle they were in was too scary for that. But the names-only part of the rules of war sounded like a good idea. He kept his mouth shut.

"How old are you, Cisco?" Ms. Cooperman repeated.

Cisco stared at his knees.

She turned to Poppy. "It looks as if the cat's got your brother's tongue. What about you, Poppy? How old are you and Barbara and Danny?"

Poppy looked at Cisco, then down at her hands in her lap. Babba, at the sound of her name, stirred and stretched and sat up.

Ms. Cooperman tried again. "Barbara, honey, how old are *you?*"

Cisco nudged Poppy. Poppy slid her hand down where Ms. Cooperman couldn't see, and pinched Babba's behind. Babba yelped, and then—as Cisco made a sign of locking his lips— sat back in grumpy silence. Danny, on Cisco's other side, wriggled closer to him.

"Hm," Ms. Cooperman said. "Well, then, Francisco, perhaps you can tell me where you lived before you moved into the camp, and what school you went to."

She waited.

"I see. Not until you get advice from your lawyer, is that it? That would be your aunt, I suppose." Ms. Cooperman gave a weary sigh, picked up the telephone, and tapped out four numbers. "All right. We'll see what we can do. But it's going to take time."

For a moment Cisco couldn't think who the aunt she had mentioned twice now was. When he realized that she meant Auntie Moss, he almost had to smother a giggle. Boo would have a fit if anyone called Auntie *her* aunt.

After a moment Ms. Cooperman spoke into the receiver. "Hello, Gloria? Is Al Hofstra up there? Good. Can you send him down to my office right away? All right. . . . Yes. . . . Thanks, Gloria."

Hanging up, Ms. Cooperman stood and went to open the office door. "Come along, then. You children can sit right out here until I've had a word with Mr. Hofstra, then he'll look after you." She pointed to a worn wooden bench beside her door.

Obediently, the children trooped out and sat down. At least, they sat, but more up than down. The bench appeared to have been chosen with teenagers in mind. Babba and Danny had to climb up and sit with their legs sticking out. Poppy and Cisco, who were small for eight and ten but too grownup to clamber aboard like babies, put their backsides against the bench and pushed themselves up onto it.

The hallway was busy, and almost as interesting as watching TV. Even Poppy, who was usually too shy to look anyone in the eye, watched everyone who passed. And everyone who walked past stared right back—probably, Cisco supposed, because of Babba, who was doing her wide-eyed Baby Barbie act. There were all sorts of passersby. There was a woman in slacks and running shoes and a T-shirt that read ESCALANTE RULES. A younger one in a pink sundress and wearing earrings that looked like Coca-Cola bottle caps went by with an armload of file folders. A skinny young man with a beard—Al Hofstra?—came down the hall and turned in to Ms. Cooperman's office. Two big boys in jeans and tank tops dawdled past looking as unhappy as if they were on their way to the dentist's. Or to the principal's office. And there was a police officer with a stringy-haired girl a year or two older than Boo who was carrying a plastic suitcase and a stuffed giraffe.

Poppy pulled at Cisco's T-shirt. "Is that girl arrested?" she whispered.

"I don't know. Maybe," Cisco whispered back. "Maybe she ran away from home."

Poppy watched the two figures down the hall. "I bet that's scary. Running away, I mean," she whispered. She nudged closer to Cisco. "Really scary."

No scarier, Cisco thought, than having your mom zonked out in the hospital and your daddy thousands of miles away, and Boo—where? But he couldn't say all that to Poppy.

"Mr. Smith? Miss Smith? And two more Smiths, I believe?" The bearded young man stuck his head out of Ms. Cooperman's office door. "Good, all present and accounted for. Me, I'm Al. Now, I bet you wouldn't say no to a dish of ice cream, would you?"

"Strawberry?" Babba asked.

"And then we can zip out to MacLaren Hall. We'll find you beds for tonight, ladies in the girls' wing, and you men in the boys' wing. But first—"

"No!" Cisco spoke so sharply that Al's eyebrows shot up in surprise.

"We have to stay together. Our mom said you weren't supposed to take us at all. Our—" Cisco was about to say "our sister," but that might only make them go looking for Boo. "Our Auntie can take care of us."

"I don't know anything about that," Al said. "Ms. Cooperman will decide what's best. But you'll be with us at least for tonight, and that means that—" He pulled a card from his pocket to check the names on it. "That means Poppy and Barbara will stay in a nice room with some other little girls, and Francisco and Danny will stay in the boys' part of the building. Okay?"

It wasn't the least bit okay. But Cisco was ready for it. When Major Bodley, the Salvation Army's director at the campground, had gone off to call the Children's Services Department, Auntie had upset his mother with a gloomy prediction that the kids would be split up and farmed out in so many directions that it would take days to get them all collected together again. It was no use getting mad at Auntie, who would only get madder right back at you. Cisco had, instead, crossed his heart three times and promised his mother he wouldn't let them get split up by *any*body. "Not nobody, not nohow," as the Wizard of Oz's doorkeeper said.

He had made a plan then and there. With no time to plot anything exciting or supersneaky, he had kept it simple.

"Come on," Al coaxed. "What do you say we go check out—"

"No!" Cisco said quickly, before Al could get to the ice cream. The ice cream was just bait. "We're staying together," he announced. With a nod to Poppy, he leaned over to whisper *"Go!"* in Danny's ear. Poppy whispered in Babba's.

They yelled.

Danny loved to yell, and he had strong lungs. Babba could do a high, shivery wail that made grownups clap their hands over their ears and moan. And since they were in a strange place, and frightened, making noise was almost as good as eating ice cream. Together they opened their mouths and tilted their heads back like little dogs howling.

YA-AA-AAAH-HH-HHHH-A-AA-AAAHH-AAGHHH!

EEEEEE-EE-eee-eeeee-eee-E-E-E-EE-EE-EEEEE!

Cisco and Poppy gritted their teeth.

In the bare, echoing hallway the noise was awful. Al Hofstra, pop-eyed with alarm, covered his ears. Then, bravely, he uncovered them and squatted down on his heels to try to calm Danny. *"It's all right,"* he tried to yell through the din. *"Nobody's going to hurt you here. Everything's going to be all right."*

Danny, his eyes screwed shut, kept right on bawling. All up and down the hallway, heads popped out of doors.

Cisco knew that when Danny had roared himself out—it would take about ten minutes—he could still shriek. Danny was a husky little boy, and Mr. Smith always joked that his lungs were made of tough top-quality elephant hide. Cisco wasn't so sure of Babba. A minute or two of wailing usually got her what she wanted. She might not be able to keep it up. Already she was red-faced and froggy-eyed. If anyone had ever held a mirror up so she could see what yowling made her look like, she probably would have shut up and never wailed again. But for now she was making such a racket that Cisco was full of admiration. He wanted to give her a big, smoochy kiss, but that would spoil the effect.

"What the *blazes* is going on out here?" The door across the hall from Ms. Cooperman's was flung open and a tall, balding man in shirtsleeves and a green tie with yellow polka dots leaned out. The sign on his door said he was George Prohasky.

"I'm having a meeting in here, and I can't hear

myself think," he roared. "Marlene! Are these yours?"

Ms. Cooperman's door opened and she leaned out, frowning, one hand cupped over the mouthpiece of her telephone, the other holding the telephone with the cord stretched out as far as it would go. She took one look at Babba and Danny and scuttled back in to hang up and get rid of the phone. A moment later, file folder in hand, she was across the hall and shouting in Mr. Prohasky's ear.

"I'm terribly sorry. They were so quiet. I don't understand . . . "

"Well, do something about it. Turn down the volume!" Mr. Prohasky bellowed.

Cisco gave a quick nudge to Danny and another to Babba. The roar and wail dropped to loud sobs and whimpers.

"It's because I told them they'd have to split up for the night," Al Hofstra said breathlessly.

"The mother's in the hospital, George." Ms. Cooperman handed Mr. Prohasky the file folder. "And it's too late in the day to find a temporary foster home for tonight. In any case, Louella Barnes over at Foster Care Licensing says they don't have anyone in their active files who could take four children."

Mr. Prohasky read rapidly through the forms in the folder. Then he looked at the children over the rims of his glasses. "All for one and one for all, eh?" His eyes narrowed thoughtfully. "Well, now—Francisco, is it?—if you can just keep the sound effects switched off and hang in there for five minutes, I may have an idea." He thrust the folder at Ms. Cooperman and turned back in to his office, pulling the door shut behind him.

Ms. Cooperman sighed. She turned to Al Hofstra. "Ours is not to reason why," she said. "You might as well go back to whatever you were doing before I sent for you. And you children can go sit on *that* bench." She pointed to the one outside Mr. Prohasky's door.

Obediently, the Smiths crossed the hall. Cisco supposed Ms. Cooperman wanted them off her hands. But that didn't seem to be the case, for she left the door to her office open and kept one dragonish eye on the children all the while she typed or telephoned or sorted through her files. Cisco didn't mind. By leaning his head back sideways as if he had fallen suddenly asleep, he could get his ear quite close to the crack of Mr. Prohasky's door. Poppy whispered to the little ones, who grew very quiet, except for Danny's shifting around on the bench. He had already been to the bathroom, so it wasn't that. He was still excited from all the yelling.

The blurry voices talking in Mr. Prohasky's room came through the crack of the door.

61

"... when your application is approved ...
splendid qualifications ..."

"... No older boys ... too noisy for Melba
Mae ..."

"... These children ... ages are they?"

"... can't be sure. My guess would ... four to
eight ..."

"... magic touch with little ones ..."

"... Two girls ... not twins, but close in age ..."

"... sort of time are we talking about?"

"... six weeks, possibly more ... sad situation ..."

Cisco went cold all over. The warm corridor
suddenly felt chillier than the frozen-food section
in the Lucky supermarket. Their mother *couldn't*
be staying in the hospital for weeks. She wasn't
really sick. She was only tired.

But there was worse to come. The deepest of
the voices went rumbling on, and Cisco couldn't
help hearing.

"... father?"

"... no information yet ... apparently walked
out ..."

At that Cisco shot off the bench in a fury and
flung himself at Mr. Prohasky's door.

"That's not true! You take that back!" he
shouted as the door crashed open against the
bookcase behind it. "Our father's got a new job,
back in Pennsylvania, and we're going to live back
there."

Sitting across the desk from the startled Mr.

Prohasky were a middle-aged man and woman as clean and crisp and shiny looking as if they had stepped out of a television commercial made to sell laundry soap and shampoo and toothpaste all at the same time. The man was tall even sitting down, and skinny, with frizzy red hair like a carrot-colored halo, and large hands folded in his lap. He wore a light tan suit and a pale blue checkered shirt and shiny cowboy boots. The woman was cheerfully plump, with a lot of shiny blond curls which she wore in a clump of curly bangs and a curly topknot. Her summer suit was the same color as the man's, her frilly blouse pale blue, and she wore a heart-shaped gold locket on a thin, shimmery chain. Her feet were tiny, but the heels on her shoes very high. And her blue eyes twinkled almost as brightly as the rings on her fingers.

Poppy and Babba and Danny peered into the office from behind Cisco, as curious as they were afraid.

The woman's eyes widened. She clapped her hands.

"Oh, the dear *dears*," she cried. "We'll take 'em!"

5

MAYBE, CISCO DECIDED, MS. COOPERMAN wasn't the Dragon Lady after all. When Mr. Prohasky popped across the hall to tell her that he had solved her problem, one of her eyebrows lifted in a way that could mean she didn't exactly like Mrs. Dickery. Or Mr. Dickery. If that was so, she couldn't be all bad.

The big, red-haired man and the frilly blond woman were Joseph D. and Melba Mae Dickery, and to hear Mr. Prohasky tell it, they were the next best thing to pepperoni pizza with extra cheese. He was already calling them J.D. and Peaches, which was what they called each other. He told Ms. Cooperman that their official approval had not come through yet, but according to the foster-care investigator checking them out, J.D. and Peaches were just the sort of prosperous foster parents the city needed more of. And since this was a special situation, he had decided to go right ahead. The last of the red tape could be tied up tomorrow. The Smith children, Mr.

Prohasky said, were going to have a great time at J.D. and Peaches' house in Hancock Park, which had a swimming pool and tennis court.

"Let's hope so," Ms. Cooperman said. But then she muttered under her breath, "When pigs fly!"

Mr. Prohasky, who was rattling on about the Dickerys' family owning a field full of oil wells in Oklahoma, didn't hear that bit.

Cisco did. He closed his eyes and prayed, hard. *Please,* could somebody come riding to the rescue—and quick? Somehow, just looking at Mr. Dickery made his mouth go all dry. And Mrs. Dickery's wide blue eyes looked at the little ones as hungrily as if they were hot fudge sundaes. Worse still, Babba was looking right back as if Mrs. Dickery were a double-decker sundae with extra peanuts on top. Just as if fifteen minutes earlier she hadn't been wailing like blue murder for her own mother.

Worst of all, Ms. Cooperman, after reading through the papers Mr. Prohasky shoved at her, gave a sigh and signed at the bottom of the last one. A frightened Cisco and Poppy, watching from the bench across the hall, saw her make a face at Mr. Prohasky's back as he returned to his own office. She looked as sour as a sack of lemons.

Mr. Prohasky paused at the bench outside his door to beam at the children. "Don't you worry," he said. "We'll have everything right and tight as a trivet in no time."

What, Cisco wondered numbly, was a trivet?

"Cisco, let's run away," Poppy urged in a quavery whisper.

Her brother looked longingly up and down the hall, but the stairway and elevator were too far off and the building too big and Babba's and Danny's legs too short.

"Where to? Besides, they'd just catch us." He scowled to keep back the tears, and tried hard to think up a new plan. *Any* plan. The trouble was, the kinds of adventures he was used to dreaming up were one-person ones. How could four of you make a run for it when six of your eight legs were so short? A klutzy caterpillar could make a better run for it.

While Mr. Prohasky was making photocopies of the papers the Dickerys had signed, Mr. Dickery took off for the elevator and the basement car park. It was shortly afterward, as the children followed Mr. Prohasky, Ms. Cooperman, and Mrs. Dickery past the rest rooms on the way to the elevator that Cisco hit on a Damage Control Plan. After a quick whisper in Poppy's ear, he hurried ahead to tug at Ms. Cooperman's shirt-tail.

"Please, miss? Danny has to go to the boys' room."

"I did go." Danny stuck his lip out.

"He has to go again," Cisco said quickly. Snatching his little brother's wrist, he gave it a hard squeeze. "He always has to go again before a car ride."

"Babba too," Poppy put in, looking scared but brave. Right there, in front of Ms. Cooperman, Mr. Prohasky, and Mrs. Dickery, she clapped her hand over Babba's mouth, because it was the only way to make sure Babba would keep it shut. "Even thinking about car rides makes her urpish," Poppy said breathlessly.

Ms. Cooperman gave them a sharp look, then shrugged. "All right. Go ahead."

Mrs. Dickery nodded her curly topknot in approval. "A very considerate child. *Such* dear children, all of them. So important for brothers and sisters to stay together. We're *so* fortunate to be able to help."

"Make it snappy, kids," said Mr. Prohasky.

In the men's room Danny pulled away from Cisco. "I already *went*," he said grumpily.

"I know," Cisco whispered. He turned the water on in the sink, the way they did in spy movies, so no one could hear if they tried to listen through the door.

"Look." Cisco leaned down close and made his voice sound more excited than scary. "There's this secret I've got to tell you. You know Vulpo, the wolf man in the 'Rodar the Robot' show on TV?"

Danny nodded.

"Well, we've got to be really, really careful. Mr. Dickery has *real fur* on his chest, like Vulpo has even when he's pretending to be a real man. You can see it where his shirt's open at the neck. And he's got hairy fur on the back of his hands like Vulpo, too. Maybe he's really okay. That's why we've got to be polite. But we've got to be *careful.* So you do exactly what I tell you. Right?"

Danny nodded eagerly. "Right," he whispered, his eyes wide.

Cisco turned off the water.

The boys were out in the hallway again in time to see Mr. Prohasky striding back to his office. A moment later Poppy emerged from the women's room with a strangely shy, shrinking Babba in tow.

Mrs. Dickery clapped her hands. She seemed to clap her hands a lot. "Now we're all set," she burbled. As she and Ms. Cooperman headed back down the hall, she called over her shoulder, "And mind, you kiddies call me 'Peachie,' now. It's J.D. and Peachie, not any stuffy old 'Mr. and Mrs.' "

"What did you tell Babba?" Cisco whispered as they followed the two women toward the elevator.

"Just the truth," Poppy breathed back. Babba, clinging to her hand, was listening anxiously. Poppy tried to look serious, but her eyes had a shy twinkle under their dark lashes. "I said Mrs. What's-her-name looks like the Cookie Witch. She *does.* Just like in this picture book we saw at the library, where she's all sweet and smiley until she's ready to bake Hansel and Gretel in her oven. I said we have to be really careful until we see how big this lady's oven is."

Cisco nodded solemnly. "*Really* careful."

J.D.'s car was a big, silver-colored Lincoln, almost the longest, most beautiful car Cisco had ever seen. The seats, puffy and squooshy, were covered with soft gray leather, and the dashboard up front had so many dials and gauges and blinking numbers that it looked like the cockpit in an airplane.

The children sat squeezed together in a silent row in the back seat. J.D. touched a button up front, and the locks on both back doors snapped shut. Ms. Cooperman, leaning down to talk with the Dickerys through Mrs. Dickery's open window, saw Cisco blink at the sound and bite his lip. She looked as if she were going to say something to him, but changed her mind and put on a grim smile instead.

To Mrs. Dickery, she said, "Thank you for taking the children on such short notice."

"Goodness sakes, you people needn't thank us, my dear," Peachie answered. "We'd be just heartsick to think of these little ones separated and crying themselves to sleep while we had beds sitting empty. And yes, we hope it's only for a night or two, too."

Poppy was right about Peachie, Cisco decided. She even had a Cookie-Witch voice, all honey and icing sugar, the better to fool you with. He was much too grown up to believe in witches and wolf men and all that little-kid stuff, but he suddenly found himself wondering how big her oven really was. As soon as the thought popped into his head, he felt silly, but he couldn't help it.

Ms. Cooperman kept a thoughtful eye on Cisco as she answered. "Yes, of course," she said. "In any case, I'll come by early tomorrow with those last papers that need signing. *And* some good news from the hospital, I hope. Sometime between nine and nine-thirty?"

"That'll be fine. Just dandy perfect. Won't it, J.D.?"

J.D. smiled a broad smile and said jokingly, "Couldn't be perfecter."

His two pointy eye teeth were *very* pointy. Danny stretched up tall to sneak a look at the two large hands resting on the steering wheel and sat back quickly. Their backs were hairy all the way to the knuckles, with light, reddish hair like a fox's.

Cisco's eyes met Ms. Cooperman's as she drew back from the window, and he felt his ears go red. Scaring Danny and Babba so all they would care about was getting back to Boo and their mom and Elvira was a mean trick, but it had been the only one he could think of. Ms. Cooperman's

70

sharp look and faint frown made him wonder if the Dragon Lady could read minds.

"Fasten your seat belts, children," Peachie said cheerily.

Gloomily, they did. There were only three belts, so Babba and Danny shared the middle one.

As the big silvery car glided down the aisle of the parked cars, Cisco craned around to look out the rear window. Ms. Cooperman stood by the elevator, watching them out of sight. Then the car turned a corner and nosed up the ramp and out into the sunlight and the bustle of traffic.

After the growl and jiggle and *tink-tunk* of Elvira, riding in the Dickerys' car felt like swishing along on silk. In what seemed no time at all the big car had slid through the downtown traffic and onto Wilshire Boulevard. Wilshire Boulevard turned out to be a wide street that went on and on and on, through a park and past big stores and hotels and office buildings.

With stores and offices closing for the day, the traffic was heavy and the going slow. Cisco had plenty of time to keep count of the street numbers, and to work out how often they passed buses heading downtown. Just in case. It was too bad that there was no way he could lay a Hansel-and-Gretel trail—not in a big city, going twenty miles or more an hour with nothing to drop out the window but a few sunflower seeds from the bottom of his jeans pocket, which beady-eyed pigeons would probably snatch on the first bounce. Besides, who was there to follow a trail even if he had a sack full of plastic tiddlywinks to flip out the window? Nobody. Still . . .

His hand reached under his T-shirt to touch his belt. He might not have any tiddlywinks, but . . .

The street numbers were already up to the 4400s, more than fifty blocks from the campground along Seventh Street, when the big silver Lincoln turned right onto Arden Boulevard and then right again. A little farther on, it turned in at a driveway lined with rose bushes. Passing the house, it drove straight on back into an open middle stall of a four-car garage.

"Wow!" Cisco marveled. *Four* cars! And the house looked as if it had maybe twenty rooms. On second thought, maybe staying just for the one night wouldn't be so bad. . . .

Maybe. Except that, as Peachie opened the rear door of the car and the Smith children slid out, J.D. was opening the side door of the big, dusty, plum-colored van in the next stall. He motioned them in.

Danny pulled away from J.D.'s hairy hand and clung to Cisco. "No. I got to go to the baffroom."

"No problem." J.D. grinned. "We've got us a 'baffroom' right here in the garage. That door over there. You give him a hand, Francisco, old buddy."

The door at the back of the garage led to a real bathroom, small, but with a shower, a toilet, and a tiny sink for washing hands. Through a little window in the rear wall, Cisco could see a swimming pool, and beyond it a paved court with a net strung across the middle: a real tennis court. But if this was J.D. and Peachie's house, where were they going to go in the van? It didn't make any sense.

By the time he and Danny came out again, the van was out of the garage and parked beside the house, waiting.

The inside of the van had been fitted out like a mini-bus, with four narrow rows of seats behind the driver's. Cisco picked the back seat. Pressing his face against the side window, he watched Peachie click-clack up the stone steps at the corner of the house to a big, arched door with fancy carving all over it. She unlocked the door, vanished inside, and a moment later reappeared with two bulging carrier bags. She locked the door, tucked the keys into a large pot of begonias, and hurried back to the van. Something about the nervous way she moved made Cisco wonder what was up.

"Aren't we at your house *yet?*" Babba whined. She drew closer to Poppy as the Cookie Witch slid open the side door and dumped the carrier bags on the floor beside their seat.

"Dear me, no," Peachie chirped as she settled

herself in the front passenger seat. She turned back to give the children another of her bright, sugary smiles. "We've got a long way to go. A *long* way."

Cisco's heart gave an alarming *thump-bump*. He had been anxious before. Suddenly he was three-fourths terrified and one-fourth excited. Oh, glurk! he thought. What if they're *stealing* us? The Big Smith Snatch!

"ALL COMFY?" PEACHIE THE COOKIE Witch cooed as the van turned up Arden Road in the opposite direction from the way they had come. "If you're hungry, there's a box of cookies in the bag under the seat." She pointed. "And seeing as you've had such a long, unhappy day, and don't feel much like talking, why don't you all take a nice, long snooze? We really do have miles and miles to go. And there's a whole seat apiece to stretch out on."

Reaching back, Peachie unfastened the cord to a rolled-up sunshade so that it dropped to cover the windows all the way along her side.

"You do the one over on your side, Poppy dear," she prompted. "Francisco can close the one on the back window. J.D. always says these nice, big side mirrors are better than the little rear-view mirror for driving."

As he reached back to pull down the sunshade, Cisco's panic passed. He began to think. If the

Cookie Witch didn't want them to see where they were going . . . well, he would see about that! He had seen enough TV and movie mysteries to know just what to do. Blindfolded kidnap victims and hostages and other captives (especially if they were detectives) knew to memorize all the turns and bumps and sounds so they could find their way back. Without a blindfold it ought to be easier than on TV.

He stretched out on the last row of seats. That way, if the Cookie Witch looked back, she could see only his feet. And between the seat back and the side wall of the van was a gap just wide enough for him to see out between the rim of the back window and the sunshade. He had to be facing the back of the seat to do it, with his shoulders scrunched up and his chin propped on the armrest. And he could slip his hand up under the side-window shade to ease that window open a crack.

But keeping track of where they went was harder than it looked on TV. There were too many turns—right, left, right, left, right, then after a while left again, then right again. After that there weren't any turns for a long while, just bends in the road now and then. And there wasn't much to see through the narrow strip of window but sky and treetops and the upper parts of buildings. The few street signs he saw zipped past too fast to read. Then, after what seemed a very long time, the van turned onto a road with a lot of curves and only treetops whipping past. There were no more stops at traffic lights either, so it had to be a freeway. He watched for overhead freeway signs, but the ones he could see all had their backs to him.

It was hopeless.

"Rise and shine, kiddies!" Peachie sang out. "Almost there!"

Cisco sat up and rubbed the crick in his neck. Poppy pulled the cord that rolled up the sunshade on her side as Peachie reached back to roll up the other.

They had left the freeway behind. Out in the sunshine, a hillside, shrubbery, and then an ordinary street of ordinary houses slid sedately past. As the van turned up a side street, here and there among the boxy one-storey houses were older and fancier two-storey ones. There were a few nice old shade trees and a tall, skinny palm tree or two, but most of the houses had no flowers out front, only grass. One, though, up ahead on Cisco's side, was almost hidden inside its own little fringe of forest.

The van slowed, and Cisco and Poppy exchanged a nervous glance. The dark house with trees all around it? Was that the Dickerys'? How could it be? J.D. and Peachie were so shiny and new and the house so shabby and shaggy. As the van rolled nearer still, some of the greenery hiding the big old house turned out to be ivy that covered the shingled walls like leafy green matting. Behind the tall wooden fence grew tall redwood trees and giant tree ferns and dark, thickety hedges. All such a house needed to make it completely creepy was a turret with a pointy top. And there were two of them! Cisco slid the window open all the way and leaned out, the better to see.

It was the best, creepiest house he had ever seen.

As J.D. spun the steering wheel and the big plum-colored van turned to pull up in front of the wide gate in the tall fence, Cisco felt a shiver of excitement. Maybe J.D. and Peachie weren't going to be so bad after all. A creepy house with creaking floorboards and secret rooms and maybe—maybe even a ghost? A ghost would be better than any big, fancy garden with a swimming pool and tennis court. In his excitement Cisco forgot all about being worried.

Poppy looked out the window and shivered too, but more as if someone had dropped an ice cube down her back.

Babba and Danny, who had really fallen asleep, stirred and stared out sleepily.

Peachie drew a small plastic box from her handbag and, holding it up, turned to smile over the seat back at Babba.

"Here we are, lovey. At J.D. and Peachie's castle! How'd you like to push the button on the magic box that opens the castle gate?"

The word *magic* must have made Babba think of cookie witches, because she shrank back against Poppy, shaking her head. "That's all right, sweetie," Peachie said. "You don't have to." And she pressed the button on the automatic gate opener herself.

"But who's going to drive in?" J.D. asked in a hearty voice as the gate swung open. "How about Danny?"

Danny's eyes widened and he tugged eagerly at his and Babba's safety-belt buckle.

"Come sit up here then, Danny-boy." J.D. held out a hairy hand.

Danny froze, his eyes on the big hand with its heavy gold ring and red-gold fuzz, then pulled his knees up to his chest and hugged them tight.

"Not interested?" J.D. laughed. He didn't seem at all bothered. "Here we go, then." And in the van rolled, to stop by a side door under a wide carporch that reached all the way across the driveway. The gate swung shut behind it. Beyond, at the end of the driveway, stood a two-stall garage. A dusty old green van was parked under the trees, off to the side of the driveway. The door to one garage stall stood open.

"Peachie," J.D. proposed as he got out and opened the door on Poppy's side, "what say you go introduce Francisco and Poppy and Barbara and Danny to the rest of the family? Our kids can give 'em the grand tour of the house while we go change."

"I didn't know they had kids," Poppy whispered in surprise.

Peachie beamed as she hopped out of the van. "Good thinking, J.D., honey. Come along, all!" she called to the Smiths as she bustled around the front end on her way to the side door. She beckoned with one glittery hand heavy with rings.

Cisco suddenly found himself in two minds about spending the night with the Dickerys. He felt guilty about forgetting why he and Poppy and the babies were in a pickle in the first place, and wished fiercely that the four of them could be safely back with their mother. Or at least with Boo. But impossible was impossible. And though J.D. and Peachie weren't exactly ordinary, they didn't behave the way kidnappers were supposed to. Since when were kidnappers friendly and cheerful? And why would they kidnap the Smiths anyhow? They couldn't pay ransom. Not even the Smith children's stubborn silence had flustered them. To tell the truth, Cisco found he wasn't sure anymore what exactly it was that had spooked him into frightening Danny with Vulpo the Wolf Man. And their house *was* great, almost as gloomy and creaky-looking as what he imagined the haunted house in *The Secret Under the Stairs* should be.

Besides, if they had kids of their own, they must be okay. The villains on TV never had kids.

Clicking along the hallway in her teetery high heels, Peachie unlocked and threw open the door into a large, shadowy room and flipped the light switch. With the lights on, the living room was a lot like almost anybody's living room. Almost. The wood floors were bare, but there were flowered drapes, bookcases, an old but comfortable-looking sofa, a coffee table with a neat stack of boxed games, Lotto and Monopoly and several others, and an assortment of armchairs.

Poppy let out a sigh of relief, but Cisco was disappointed. He had expected old-fashioned furniture, heavy velvet curtains, and creaky floor-boards, to match the house's storybook-spooky outside. Instead, it was all just . . . ordinary.

A shrill, earsplitting *Peep-peep-peeep-peeeeeeeep!* like the shriek of a smoke alarm echoed through the house.

Cisco jumped, Poppy squeaked, and Babba and Danny looked as if they might start up their screaming act again.

"It's all right, it's all right." Peachie laughed, waving the children on in. "Nothing to worry about. Just one of our silly games."

Cisco looked around gloomily. But then Poppy gave a yelp, and his frown vanished. Looking where she pointed, he heard a creaking sound in one section of the tall wooden cupboards along

81

the back wall. Then one cupboard trembled and slowly swung outward. The Smiths stood astonished as a small horde of children poured out through the opening with shouts of "Peachie, Peachie!"

There was so much noise and confusion that at first it seemed as if there must be a dozen of them, but then Peachie frowned and held up a hand. At once the strange children fell silent and lined up at attention in front of her, and it turned out that there were only seven.

They did not look much like brothers and sisters. The tallest was a girl of about thirteen, and there was a boy who looked about ten, like Cisco, though he was taller. Next in line were a girl and boy who might be seven, and three small boys about Babba's age. Danny and Babba in their curiosity forgot all about wolf men and witches with ovens, and though Poppy drew back shyly, her worried frown vanished. Cisco, whose heart had been going *bim-bim-bim-bim-bim* as the cupboard creaked open, was more disappointed than ever. The children were as ordinary as the living room.

Still, it *was* peculiar. The children, like the house, were somehow ordinary and weird at the same time. Cisco couldn't decide why. They were dressed all alike in jeans and identical blue T-shirts with white stripes. There was nothing really funny-odd in that. And their lineup for inspection was funny as in giggle-silly more than funny-peculiar.

Peachie went down the line looking as stern as Coach Simmons at Pee-Wee League ball practice. She inspected faces and fingernails and the fronts of T-shirts. Everyone must have passed, because she held out her arms and they rushed her, getting hugs all around.

"Please, please, can we play Snatch?" the littlest ones clamored.

Babba, before Poppy could pull her back, ran to get in on the hugs too. Peachie wrapped her arms around her and beamed at Cisco over her shoulder.

"Isn't she just the *dearest* little thing?" Peachie cried.

It was hard to be sure, but there might have been a shadow of a smirk in her smile.

"Snatch! Snatch!" the younger children cried excitedly. "Can we play Snatch? Can we?"

"Not now," Peachie snapped, but she quickly smiled again. "We'll see." She clapped her hands. "Listen-up time!"

Everyone was quiet.

"Children, meet Francisco, Poppy, Barbara, and Danny Smith. Smiths, this noisy bunch is—" She pointed as she recited the names. "These three little monkeys are Harry, Sam, and Chuckie. Tim and Tina, the two in the middle, are twins. Here is George. And this is Sugar." She nodded at the big girl. "Now, Sugar, you show the Smiths around. Supper at six-thirty. Off you go." With a clatter of high heels she vanished through a door nearby.

Poppy and Cisco looked at each other uncertainly, but Babba and Danny were already trooping off with the other children in Sugar's wake. The two older Smiths followed, puzzled. For the strange children were still as quiet as if Peachie had put a spell on them. Once she was gone, they didn't yell or jump around. When they talked, they whispered. And they watched the Smith children out of the corners of their eyes as if they were afraid the Smiths might go off like firecrackers. As Sugar led the way around the house, they followed behind like the tail of a silent, twitchy crocodile.

The inside of the house turned out to be every bit as interesting as its outside, but not in the way Cisco had expected. Hiding behind the doors of the tall cupboards in the living room were a compact-disc player, a double tape deck, quadruple speakers, *two* kinds of VCRs, a giant-screen television set, and shelf after shelf of video tapes and music tapes and discs.

"Oh, wow!" Cisco stared.

"We won them playing Snatch," one of the small boys piped proudly.

"Shut up, Chuckie." Sugar gave the little boy a sharp nudge.

84

Each room Sugar showed them was brightly painted—even the floors—each in a different color. The dining room and all the furniture in it were green, with a dark green floor and an apple-green ceiling and pea-green table. To Cisco it felt like being inside a lettuce. In the yellow kitchen there were *two* microwave ovens, a fancy countertop electric grill, a mixer, a juicer and blender, and a counter full of other appliances the Smiths had seen before only in magazines and on TV. A big, old, restaurant-size refrigerator stood in one corner. The stove was huge too, with six burners and an oven more than twice as large as any of the Smiths had ever seen.

Babba froze in front of the oven.

Poppy too. She looked as if she didn't know whether to giggle or start worrying. With a big enough pan, it could easily roast a small Hansel *and* a Gretel.

From the kitchen, Sugar led the way up to the bedrooms, not by the wide stairs in the front hall, but by the "back" stairs behind one of the living-room cupboards. J.D., Sugar said proudly, had built the cupboard himself and rigged it to swing out like a door. The door at the top opened onto a small landing, from which a second door opened out into the upstairs hall. The stairs, Cisco thought excitedly, would make a great hiding place. Any stranger looking in from the hall would take the landing for a closet. There was even a clothes rod with coats hanging on it. Cisco almost hugged himself in his delight. A secret staircase more than made up for all the ordinary furniture. It *almost* made up for having to spend a night away from Boo and his mom.

Four of the bedrooms were furnished with two sets of bunk beds each. "This'll be yours," Sugar said as they looked into the fourth. The fifth, which Sugar said was J.D.'s "office," was locked, as was the sixth.

"Is that Mr. and Mrs. Dickery's room?" Poppy asked shyly.

Sugar snorted and gave her a how-dumb-can-you-be? look. "Who are Mr. and Mrs. Dickery? If you mean Mom and Pop, our name's Dockett, not Dickery. And you're s'posed to call them J.D. and Peachie. All the foster kids do."

Cisco looked around the circle of faces. "All of you are foster kids?"

"Just them. Not me," Sugar said smugly as she set off down the hall. "We got George in Oklahoma and the twins in Texas, and the Three Monkeys in Arizona. Come on. There's lots more to see."

One of the two large bathrooms had an entire wall almost covered with towels on towel rods, and a rack full of electric toothbrushes on the wall beside the sink. The other, J.D. and Peachie's, had bigger, softer towels, and a trim little bathroom scale that talked. Really talked. Sugar stepped on it and a weird computer voice in the scale spoke up and said, *"One hundred and two pounds, and two ounces."* It was as eerie as—as a talking harp in a fairy tale. Sugar let each of the Smith children take a turn on it.

The big attic playroom was even better. It had climbing ropes, a large homemade jungle gym, balance beams, and tangles of fat plastic pipe for squirming through.

Danny's eyes were like saucers. Babba's too.

"It's for playing Snatch," one of the little boys piped up.

"For practicing for it," the twin Tina said.

"What's Snatch?" Cisco asked. "A game? I never heard of it."

The younger children bounced and jiggled, bursting to tell, but no one answered. Sugar pretended she hadn't heard.

"Who wants to try the tunnel?" George asked nervously.

Danny was inside and wriggling around the first bend when suddenly a loud *GONG-G-G!* sounded. By the second gong the other children had vanished without a sound. As a third *GONG-G-G-G!* echoed around the playroom, Danny was still inside the pipe. When at last he wriggled out at the far end, the four Smiths clattered down the uncarpeted stairs after the others.

In the green dining room Peachie and J.D. and the children were already seated in their green chairs at the long green table. Along its middle were platters heaped with hamburgers in their buns, big bowls of salad and French fries, four bottles of catsup, and three big pitchers of lemonade.

Peachie waggled a finger at the four Smiths. "Late, late, late," she sang out. "But don't you worry. Late doesn't count the first time. You just sit yourselves down right here, Barbara next to me, and we'll be all set." She waved a hand at the four empty chairs to her left.

"Everybody tuck in your napkins and help yourselves," J.D. boomed. He beamed at the big steak and mound of potatoes on his own plate. "Looks real good, Peachie."

Cisco forgot everything but how hungry he was. He ate three hamburgers and some French fries. And a bowl of salad, since it had blue-cheese dressing. And drank two glasses of lemonade. Afterward, he ate a big dish of fudge brownie ice cream, but he was so full that it was hard work.

Danny, with a catsup drip on his chin, was in seventh heaven. No one made him eat salad, and Peachie gave him seconds on ice cream.

Babba, after eating a hamburger without the bun, and three forkfuls of salad, took *three* servings of ice cream. Even Poppy, who was only a nibbler, ate a whole hamburger and finished her salad and a bowl of ice cream.

"Hurrah for Poppy!" Peachie clapped her

hands with their glittery rings. "Give us a few days and we'll start to fatten her up."

Babba, remembering that the Cookie Witch in the storybook kept poking Hansel and Gretel to test whether they were fat enough to roast in her oven, put down her spoon and left the last of her ice cream to melt in her bowl.

After their huge meal, the long, hard day caught up with the four Smiths. As they sat watching "Double Dare" on the giant TV in the living room, even Cisco kept dropping off to sleep. Shooed upstairs by Peachie to get ready for bed, they found four fresh new pairs of pajamas stacked on their bedroom chair, with four new toothbrushes on top. It felt almost like being inside a fairy tale. First Poppy and Babba took a shower and brushed their teeth, then Cisco and Danny. Showers were *much* nicer than bathtubs, and the toothpaste came out of the tube in red and white stripes.

Babba and Danny tumbled into the two bottom bunks and were asleep almost before Poppy could pull their covers up. Cisco and Poppy, on the top bunks, were almost too tired to whisper.

"That must be the best TV set in the whole world." Cisco gave a happy sigh as he punched a comfortable dent in the middle of his pillow and burrowed further down between the sheets. "It's not so bad here after all. Maybe we'll get to stay tomorrow night too."

"Mm-mm-hm." Poppy yawned. But she didn't fall asleep right away. One silly, Babba-ish thought kept niggling her awake. *They're trying to fatten us up. They're trying to fatten us up.*

The clock atop the bookcase by the window said two o'clock when Cisco awoke. The room was warm and stuffy. "Mom forgot to open the window," he thought fuzzily as he struggled to sit up. He sat rubbing his eyes.

The window was in the wrong place. Why was the window in the wrong place?

"Momma?" he whispered. Frightened, he pulled his legs up to his chest and rocked back and forth, hugging his knees. "Momma?" And then, dimly, he saw the bunk bed against the other wall and knew where he was.

At that, Cisco felt like putting his head down on his knees to cry, but he didn't dare. If the babies woke up, that would really scare them. And if everybody started blubbering, Peachie might come to see what was the matter. He didn't want that. Besides, it would all be OK. Tomorrow—today—Ms. Cooperman was coming, and she would say their mom was fine, and everything was going to be okay.

Slipping quietly down the bunk ladder, Cisco padded across to the window in his bare feet and opened the curtains. There were shutters too, and he had to feel around for the catch, but once the shutters were open, the moonlight spilled in and Cisco could see the lock on the window itself.

He could also see most of the driveway below, and the garage at the back of the house—and the dark shape of a van slowly rolling out from under the carporch that arched across the driveway just below and to the right of the window. Easing the window up a tiny crack, he heard the soft rumble of the front gate closing.

Cisco dropped to his knees and very slowly raised his head above the windowsill, just high enough to see.

The van, its headlights dark, crept to a soundless stop just outside of the garage.

As Cisco watched, a dark, humpy figure, with seven smaller humps of shadow following at its heels, separated itself from the dark bulk of the van. As they melted into the shrubbery, the van, with its headlights still out, rolled forward and disappeared into the blackness of the open garage.

Talk about *weird*.

Once the shutters were closed and the curtains drawn again, Cisco pinched himself to make sure he was awake. He still felt fuzzy-headed, and the scene in the moonlight had been as silent and strange as a dream.

The pinch hurt. But just to be sure, he tiptoed across to the door for a peek into the room across the hall. If George and the Three Monkeys were there, he was still dreaming.

The door handle wouldn't turn.

Cisco tried again. Still it wouldn't turn.
They were locked in.

Behind him, Poppy made a funny sort of
squeak and turned restlessly in her sleep. "Zisco,"
she mumbled, the words muffled in her pillow,
" 's really is d'cookie house."

7

AUNTIE MOSS SAT SNOOZING IN THE corner of one of the hospital-lobby sofas. Even cleaned up and wearing just one sweater over her rumpled blouse and an old, tight pair of sandals instead of dirty tennis shoes, she was embarrassing. Her head was tilted back against the orange plastic cushion and her mouth hung open. Her snore was only a soft little bumblebee of a sound, but every once in a while she let out a snort and twitched all over, like an old dog does when it's dreaming. Every time, Boo blushed and snuck a look around the lobby to see if anyone had noticed.

Mostly, no one had. Several other people were stretched out asleep on sofas or slumped in armchairs, watching TV. Boo had seen a few of them the afternoon before, when she and Auntie had first tried to see her mother. A middle-aged man and woman, with pillows under their heads and blankets straggling to the floor, looked as if they had come prepared and spent all night right there.

Boo wished she had stayed all night, too. But both the receptionist behind her glass window in the lobby and then a nurse from Mrs. Smith's corridor upstairs had said that the doctor's orders were "Absolutely no visitors allowed." So Auntie had insisted on going back to the campground and returning to the hospital in the morning. In the morning, according to the nurse, the doctors made their visits to the patients. In the morning Mrs. Moss and Boo could ask the doctor himself about Mrs. Smith. And there would be someone in the Social Assistance Office who would know whether the social workers had contacted Mr. Smith in Pittsburgh.

Auntie had jumped at that. She had been as fidgety as a cat with fleas from the moment they first walked through the front door of the Women's Hospital division of the giant county hospital. "Yes, ma'am. That's just what we'll do, ma'am," she said, and dragged Boo off in the direction of the elevator before Boo could protest.

Auntie never would have agreed to stay overnight in the waiting room. Not even if she'd known it was allowed. "Hospitals give me the willies," she said. And besides, all the way back to the campground she had fretted about her precious bundles. How could she be sure Mr. Allison was really keeping an eye on them? As if, Boo grumbled to herself, anybody would want to burgle a bunch of beat-up trash bags full of old clothes.

This morning the trash bags were safely stowed in the back of Elvira and locked in.

Auntie, with that excuse for fretting gone, fell to fretting about why the doctor hadn't come, and about how hospitals were crawling with germs, and about how she wasn't used to getting up at the crack of dawn and tooting off without a decent breakfast. A peanut-butter-and-jelly sandwich didn't count. But after Boo had found a coffee machine and brought a cup of sugared black coffee back to her, she settled down to a low grumble. And finally fell asleep.

Nine fifty-five, the clock on the waiting-room wall said.

Nine fifty-five? Boo's mother *never* slept past eight o'clock, not even on Sundays. No matter how tired she was.

Boo went back upstairs, trying hard to look as tall as any other twelve-year-old. Under-twelve visitors weren't welcome, one nurse had explained, because they might be carrying germs for measles or chicken pox or mumps—especially measles, which were dangerous for grownups. She crossed from the elevator to the swinging doors that opened onto the corridor that led to the ward where her mother's bed was, and pushed them open to peer down the long hallway for the eleventh or twelfth time.

Except for the nurse talking on the telephone

at the nurses' station, there wasn't a white uniform in sight. And that one nurse had her back turned.

Boo didn't even stop long enough to decide whether to make a dash for her mother's ward or not.

She just dashed.

At least four of the nurses were *in* the ward. One was pushing a cupboardish-looking thing on wheels from bed to bed, checking names on a list and handing out pills in little plastic cups. Two were lifting an old woman into bed. And the other one was down by the screened-off bed at the far end of the room, talking with a doctor. Boo hoped that bed wasn't her mother's.

For an awful minute she was afraid it was. In each of the other beds where she couldn't see the patient's face, the shapes under the sheets were all wrong. But there was a bed in the near corner. It was screened off like the one at the far end, with a white nylon curtain that ran in a track fastened to the ceiling. Boo stuck her head through the opening, and then slipped inside.

Her mother lay fast asleep on the high bed, on her side, with her knees pulled as far up to her chest as her baby-big tummy would let them go. Tummy and all, she looked almost too small to be a grownup. Even her face looked young. All the worry lines were gone, and the corners of her mouth twitched upward once or twice, as if she were dreaming about something nice. The house in Pittsburgh, maybe. Or Daddy.

Boo put her hand on her mother's arm and jiggled it. *"Mom,"* she whispered.

But it was a deep voice that answered her, from outside the curtain.

"What tiny feet you have, Nurse!" it rumbled.

Boo jumped, then jiggled her mother's arm harder as the doctor who had been down at the far end of the ward swept the curtains open. "Mom, wake up!" she yelped.

Mrs. Smith only stirred and made a high, soft *Unnnh* sound in her sleep.

"Oh, no you don't, young lady!" The doctor took Boo firmly by the elbow and hustled her toward the hall. One of the nurses swished the curtain shut and bustled after them.

"Leave her to me, Dr. Bachman. I'll call Security," the nurse said grimly. "They'll find out who she came in with. You don't have—"

"Time? No, I don't have time to waste on silly children who can't read signs." The doctor scowled down at Boo. "I have something like thirty more patients to look in on before lunch. What's your name, Shorty?"

Boo reddened. She hated being called Shorty.

"Boo—Belinda Smith. And I came with Auntie. She's downstairs in that waiting-room place. I promise I'll go down and stay there, but—"

"Boobelinda? That's a new one on me." The doctor grinned. "Okay, you do that, Boobelinda.

97

And when I'm finished here, I'll come down on my way to lunch to talk to you and your auntie about your mother. Now, scram, or Nurse Cassidy *will* call Security."

Boo scrammed.

"I see," Dr. Bachman said when he joined them in the lobby. "The 'Boo' is only for short. Well, that's a relief. I've heard some pretty peculiar names in my time, but Boobelinda would have taken the cake." He sounded perfectly serious, but the twitch at the corners of his mouth gave him away. He must have known all along.

He was very serious when he turned to Auntie, though.

"I'll explain your niece's condition as simply as I can, so that Boo will understand how very important it is that she rest. We mustn't allow anything to upset her. We think she has what we call 'pre-eclampsia,' but we won't know for sure until we hear from the laboratory about some tests that we've done. If we're right, then she's going to have to stay in bed until September, when the baby's due. Otherwise things could be very bad for both of them."

Boo felt numb. Stay in *what* bed until September?

"You've probably noticed the swelling in your mother's ankles, and that she's been having a lot of headaches."

Boo nodded. She had known something was wrong. She had *known* it.

"Well, her blood pressure is higher than we like to see, too. All this probably means that she's been working too hard, or has been worrying about something until she's exhausted herself. She told the doctor who saw her first that everything was fine, but the nurse who was there when the first shot wore off said that she was like a wound-up rubber band. That's why we had to give her something to put her to sleep. You tell me: *Does* she work too hard? Or worry a lot?"

Auntie snorted. "Do birds fly? Do pigs eat?"

Boo looked at Dr. Bachman, hard. He was shorter than her father, and younger even though his dark hair was already a little bit thin on top. But he had the same way of tilting his head and looking as if he was going to be really interested in whatever you said. It was that look that decided Boo.

She told him everything: about Pittsburgh, the day-care kids, the disappointing garage sale, the campground—everything, that is, except about Auntie's being a fake aunt.

When she finished, Dr. Bachman sighed. "Sweetie," he said, "this place is full of stories like that." He scribbled on a page of his pocket notebook, then tore out the sheet and handed it to Auntie.

"This is who you should talk to: Mrs. Domingo,

in the Social Service office. Ask the receptionist to explain to you where that is. Mrs. Domingo's probably been in touch with Mr. Smith already, and she'll be able to find out for you where the other children have been taken."

"But when's Mom going to wake up?" Boo asked anxiously. "When can I see her?"

"Tomorrow morning. All right? We want to keep her asleep until then, and after that she'll get a pill every eight hours to keep her relaxed and just a little bit sleepy. *But.* I don't want her to hear anything that's going to worry her. You're not to let on that you children have been split up. Just tell her the rule is 'no visitors under twelve years old.' Agreed?"

Boo nodded again, glumly.

Mrs. Domingo peered at her computer terminal. "No, we have no next of kin listed for Mrs. Smith. But there's a note on the file that she refused to name any. From what Belinda tells me, I would guess that means she didn't want us worrying Mr. Smith about her—or the bills." She drew a deep breath. "But, if there's no home here for her to go home to, it sounds as if she's going to be with us for a long time. I'll call the Red Cross right away, and they'll get through to their Pittsburgh office. It shouldn't take them long to find your father, Belinda. And I'll call the County Children's Services people and find out what arrangements they've made for your brothers and sisters."

Auntie, instead of being uneasy at the mention of the county social workers, seemed almost relieved. She had been very quiet after Dr. Bachman took her aside for a private word. Boo watched her as they waited in the outer office while Mrs. Domingo made her phone calls. She even looked oddly different today. Her clothes weren't so awful, and her hair was pulled back almost neatly into a stubby gray ponytail, but that wasn't it. And then, suddenly, Boo saw what it was.

"Hey, your teeth! You've got all your teeth."

"You don't hafta shout it from the rooftop," Auntie muttered. "It's no big deal. I found my bridge in this old handbag, that's all." She fanned herself for a moment with a tattered copy of *TIME* from the table beside her and then said, "Tell you what. We can go out after while and fix some of your peanut-butter sandwiches for lunch, then come back and hang around until they track your daddy down. Maybe I'll read me some of these old magazines. How does—"

She broke off as the outer door swung open and a frizzy-haired woman in a blue dress burst in. Her eyes swept around the office, fixed on Auntie with a faint, puzzled frown, and then settled on the secretary sitting at the desk nearest the door.

101

"Is—" The woman looked at a piece of paper she held. "Is Betty Domingo in?"

The secretary nodded. "Yes. But she's—"

"Is that her office?" The woman indicated the door to Mrs. Domingo's cubicle and, when the secretary nodded again, reached for the doorknob and strode right in.

"Yes, but—" The secretary blinked as the door banged shut. Scrambling out of her chair, she followed, opened the door cautiously, and stuck her head in. "I'm sorry, Mrs. Domingo. Shall I . . ."

Mrs. Domingo must have said it was all right, because the secretary closed the door again and returned to her desk with a shrug. Auntie, frowning, gave Boo a sharp nudge.

"That's her," she hissed.

" 'Her'? *Who?*"

"The one from Children's Services. The one who came to the camp and took the kids. Name of Kupperman. Hooperman. Something like that."

A moment later, Mrs. Domingo herself was in the doorway.

"Mrs. Moss? Belinda? I think you had better come in."

Inside, Mrs. Domingo motioned to them to sit down again. "I've talked to the Red Cross, Mrs. Moss," she said. "They're calling Pittsburgh right away. And it seems I don't need to phone the Children's Services Department after all. This is their Ms. Cooperman. She says she's come about your little ones, and I've been explaining that if there's a problem she'll have to talk with you, since she can't see Mrs. Smith."

Ms. Cooperman gave Auntie and Boo a blank stare. "Mrs. . . . Moss? I don't . . . Oh, yes, the great-aunt. I'm sorry. I didn't recognize you, Mrs. Moss. And I didn't know . . . "

"What problem?" Boo demanded quickly. "Where are the kids?"

"Oh, dear. Oh, dear!" Ms. Cooperman looked at Boo unhappily. "I wish I'd known there were five of you. I don't know what I could have done, but—" She took a deep breath. "Well, to make a long story short, in order to keep the children together, we placed them in a temporary foster home. I went out to Chiltern Place in Hancock Park this morning to get the foster parents' signatures on some forms, and to see how the children were settling in. And . . . "

"*And?*" Auntie demanded. "For Pete's sake, don't gargle all around it, woman. Spit it out!"

Ms. Cooperman took a deep breath. "I'm *trying* to. I found out that—well, it turns out that the foster parents don't even live in the house on Chiltern Place, let alone own it. The owners are in Europe for the summer. These people were hired last month as part-time caretakers. And now they've up and"—her voice wavered—"vanished."

She ran a nervous hand through her frizzy hair.

"I don't know any other way to put it," she said. "Francisco and Poppy and Barbara and Danny—they've vanished too."

8

" . . . AND SO, THEIR NAME WASN'T Dickery at all," Ms. Cooperman said breathlessly.

She sank back wearily into an armchair. "The real Dickerys are the owners of the Chiltern Place house, and they're in France for the summer. That's why, with them away and their part-time housekeeper and gardener showing up at the Foster Care offices and pretending to *be* them, everyone was so completely taken in. The credit investigation, the home inspection, they got top marks on everything because it was the real Dickerys who were being checked out."

"Huh!" Auntie snorted. "Some investigators!"

Ms. Cooperman shook her head wearily. "Our people do their best with the time they have. But we're so understaffed that we all have too many cases and never have a chance to get caught up."

She stood with a sigh.

"And I've been falling further behind all morning. I've got to grab a sandwich somewhere and get back to the office right away. I'll try to keep in touch with Mrs. Domingo here at the hospital, and with you, Mrs. Moss, through the administrative office at the campground."

"Don't be a goose! Of course it isn't all your fault," Auntie snapped when they reached Elvira's parking place. She took the keys from Boo and opened the van's side door. "So what if you did stay a while at the Maldonados? Sure, if you'd left half an hour earlier you'd have got back in time. Back in time to get whisked off with the rest of the brats, and you'd be missing now too. What good would that do Hazel Baker's pig?" Tugging out the food box, she plopped it down on top of the mattress.

"I'd be wi-ith them," Boo sniveled. She tore off half a paper towel from the roll in the box to wipe her tears and then her nose. "*What* pig? Who's Hazel Baker?"

"For Pete's sake, it's just an expression." The old woman waved an impatient hand. "Sure you'd be with 'em. And then who would have gone around sticking her nose in where she wasn't supposed to and getting that Mrs. Domingo and the Red Cross in on the act? Not me. Your dad wouldn't be hearing a thing until after your mom wakes up tomorrow. And she'd wake up with no kids." Auntie scowled as she rummaged through the box. "Good gravy! Don't you folks have *any-*

thing in here *but* brown bread and grape jelly and peanut butter?"

Boo stuffed the wad of paper towel into the sack that had WASTE PAPER written on it. Auntie was right. It was lucky that she and the kids weren't all in the same pickle. It would be worse than scary for her mother to wake up and have nobody. Boo cheered up a little. The thought of peanut-butter-and-jelly sandwiches helped too.

"That's not the way." She took the knife away from Auntie. "You put on too much jelly. It'll squoosh out and dribble down your front if you put on that much."

Mrs. Domingo had said to come back at half past one, so Boo and Auntie had more than an hour to fiddle away. After two sandwiches apiece, they went indoors in search of a drinking fountain and then the women's room.

Boo didn't have to go. Instead, she locked the door to her cubicle, sat down on the seat lid, and pulled from her shoulder bag the blue plastic pencil case she had slipped out of the patchwork bag her mother had hidden under Elvira's passenger seat. The garage-sale money was in it, all right. And more. Two hundred and seven dollars in all. It held a wad of folded-up papers, too, fastened together with a rubber band. There was barely time to peek at the top two, which turned

107

out to be Poppy's birth certificate and Mr. and Mrs. Smith's wedding certificate. Boo took out three five-dollar bills and then, adding her father's check to the rest of the money, stuffed it and the papers back into the little blue case. Feeling for the tear in the lining of her shoulder bag, she carefully worked the case through it. With the torn seam neatly tucked under, no one looking into the bag would guess the case was there. Boo wasn't worried anymore about Auntie stealing it. It was just that if she knew it was there, she would grumble even more loudly about the peanut butter sandwiches and want to spend some on burgers and fries or apple pie and coffee.

At the sound of the electric hand-dryer roaring Auntie's hands dry, Boo slid the lock open and hurried out to wash her own. Later, while Auntie snoozed away the last half hour until one-thirty, she went exploring and found the hospital shop. Its shelves and tables were crowded with paperback books and stuffed animals and boxes of candy, but Boo saw nothing her mother would like. Or anyway, nothing but a get-well card with a cute white Scottie puppy on it. But it cost a dollar and twenty-five cents.

Mrs. Domingo was waiting with good news when Boo and Auntie arrived in her office at one-thirty. Her door was open, and the secretary told them to go right in.

"We're in luck," she told Boo. "There must be only the one box factory in Pittsburgh, because the Red Cross there reached your daddy on their first try."

"When? What did he say? Can I call him?" The words tumbled over each other trying to get out. Boo was so excited that she almost knocked over the potted fern on the corner of Mrs. Domingo's desk.

Mrs. Domingo smiled. "He phoned here just before I got back from lunch, and left a message that he was going to try to reach Ms. Cooperman and would call here again at about two o'clock our time."

"Two o'clock!" Boo gave a despairing look at the clock on the wall. Twenty-five whole minutes!

"Don't get your socks in a twist," Auntie snapped. She made a quick dab at her eyes with a rumpled tissue and tried to sound as if she couldn't possibly be relieved because of course she hadn't been worried at all. "It'll be two o'clock before you know it."

"That's right," Mrs. Domingo agreed. "And in case he phones before two, you'd better stay put in the outer office. I'll have the secretary send you in as soon as the call comes through."

Auntie was wrong. Two o'clock took forever to come.

When at last it did, and the telephone rang,

109

Boo zoomed off the outer-room sofa like a shot from a Roman candle.

"Social Services," the secretary answered. "Long distance from Mr. Daniel Smith for Mrs. Domingo? Just a moment. I'll put you through."

In a flash Boo was through the door and hanging across Mrs. Domingo's desk.

Mrs. Domingo held up a warning hand and went on talking. "Yes. . . . I understand that she's going to be fine, so long as she gets enough rest. I know you'll have questions for the doctor. I'll give you his phone number after you've had a word with a young lady I have here."

Boo snatched the receiver. "Daddy!" she shrieked.

"It's okay, honey." Mr. Smith's voice sounded as if he were in the outer office, not more than two thousand miles away. "Everything's going to be okay. I'm coming. Not tomorrow, but Saturday or Sunday for sure. I just talked to Granny, and she says she has enough put by in her savings account to pay for the plane ticket."

"Oh, Daddy!" Boo cried, and turned to announce, "He's coming Saturday! He's coming! When on Saturday?" she called into the telephone.

"I don't know yet. Maybe Sunday. Listen, honey. Your Mrs. Domingo says Mom's going to be all right, but I want you to tell me. Have you seen her? How does she look? And how did you and the kids get separated?"

110

Boo described her visit to the hospital ward, and then told how she had gone back to the Maldonados' house for the check that had been so late in coming. " . . . and Mrs. Maldonado made me a chicken sandwich because all I had for lunch was a peanut-butter one on the bus. So I stayed, and missed the next b-b-bus," she wailed.

"Bup-bup-bup! Hush up, now! That was *good* luck. God bless Mrs. Maldonado's chicken sandwiches! It's—it's awful about the kids, but I'm sure everything's going to be all right. And none of it's your fault, Boo. But tell me now, what's all this about somebody's aunt? That social worker, that Ms. Cooperman, kept talking about 'your aunt,' but I was so worried about the kids that it didn't register until after I hung up."

"Uh . . . " Boo's mind raced. There was no way she could explain why she had adopted Auntie as a real aunt. Not with Mrs. Domingo sitting right there, and Ms. Cooperman's name and phone number on the note pad in front of her. The anxious look on Auntie's face as she leaned forward, perched on the edge of her chair and twisting her handbag handles together, was no help either.

"Uh," Boo said carefully, "Auntie Moss is right here. She drove me over to the hospital in Elvira. When we couldn't start back to Pennsylvania, Mom got the idea of going to the campground from Auntie. She helped a lot."

There was a silence at the other end of the line,

and then Mr. Smith said slowly, "That was good of her. What are you trying to tell me, Boople? That I'd better wait and hear the whole story when I see you? Okay, okay. You don't need to say anything more. What I'm going to do as soon as I hang up is call the Maldonados and fix it up for you to stay at their house. Maybe Mr. Maldonado won't mind driving over to pick you up at the hospital."

"No," Boo said quickly. "It's okay. Auntie can drive me over in Elvira."

"Elvira . . ." her father said vaguely, as if he'd forgotten all about the van. "Yes, you're right. She'll have to park it on the street in front, and you make sure she gives Mr. Maldonado the keys." He took a deep breath. "Look, honey, I'm almost out of quarters, so I can't talk to your Mrs. Domingo again. Anyhow, it's after five here, and I've got to go catch my boss before he goes home. Maybe he'll hold my job for a couple of weeks, maybe not. But I'll see you on the weekend no matter what. At the Maldonados'. You be good, honey."

"I love you, Daddy," Boo said quickly, holding the receiver close.

"Love you too," came the answer, and then there was only a buzz on the line.

"I thought your daddy told you I was s'posed to take you over to the Maldonados' house,"

Auntie objected as she tugged Elvira's door open. "What do you need a map for? This here is Griffin Avenue. If we go straight on at the corner and along up to the Avenue Fifty-two bridge, we're almost there."

"No. There's somewhere we've got to go first." Boo's voice was muffled as she bent down to grope under the driver's seat for the old county street directory her father kept there.

Auntie, still standing in the street, gave her a suspicious glare. "What bee have you got in your bonnet now?"

Boo sat back and opened the map book across her lap. "Daddy sounded awful worried about the kids," she said innocently. "So . . . " Finding the index at the back of the book, she thumbed through the pages until she came to the Cs.

"So?"

Auntie hoisted herself into the driver's seat and leaned over to watch Boo's forefinger slide down the columns of Chestnuts, Chevy Chases, Cheyennes, Chicagos, Chicos, and Chicopees to Chile Street and Chilham Lane to Chiltern Place.

"Chiltern Place?" Auntie frowned. "Where in blazes is that?"

"Page forty-three, section one-C," Boo read aloud.

Page forty-three was just before the page for downtown, but it was like a foreign country to Boo. The name Hancock Park was written across

113

the neighborhood in section 1-C. She had never heard of it before Ms. Cooperman mentioned it. Her finger traced the streets until it came, off Arden Road, to Chiltern Place.

Chiltern Place. That was it. That was where Ms. Cooperman said the real Dickerys lived.

"So," Boo finished, "we're going looking for clues."

9

"IN A PIG'S EYE WE ARE!" AUNTIE EX-
ploded.

Boo blinked. The explosion startled her because Auntie hadn't been rude all day. For a
change. But Boo's mind was made up.

"We are so," she answered firmly. "I sure won't
go fidget away the rest of the afternoon sitting
on Mrs. Maldonado's front steps chewing my
fingernails. Not when Poppy and Cisco and
the babies are maybe shut up in a dungeon
somewhere."

Auntie snorted. "Dungeon, my foot."

"Well, a basement, then. They *could* be."

Auntie shifted uneasily in her seat. "Yeah, well,
but . . . You don't want to get in the cops' way. If
they've been out there, they've already found all
the clues. They know all about that stuff."

"But they don't know Cisco," Boo objected. "So
they probably wouldn't even *see* a Cisco clue. He's
always watching all those detective shows and old

movies on TV, like Sherlock Holmes, and the Chinese guy with the funny hat. So I bet he'll be leaving clues all over the place."

Auntie wasn't convinced, but she reached over to take the map book from Boo. "What makes you think that Cisco would know those folks were up to something fishy? To hear that Miz Koopman—okay, Cooperman—tell it, the pair of them were slick as a silver whistle." She peered at page forty-three. "Where's this place you want to go, anyhow?"

Boo reached over to point.

"Clear out there? That's no good. That's Hancock Park. It's so snooty out there they'd call the cops as soon as they saw a beat-up old heap like this come steaming down the street."

"Don't be silly," Boo said. "They can't arrest you for having an old car."

"Maybe not," Auntie admitted grudgingly. "But they sure can hassle you. It's like what some of your old neighbors say about my wagon. 'It brings down the tone of the neighborhood.' So they call the cops. If the cops come, maybe they're nice enough, but they say 'Better move along, granny. We don't want any trouble.' "

While she grumbled, Auntie started Elvira up and made her way out through the parking lot. To Boo's relief, Auntie turned back down Mission Road the way they had come, heading for downtown.

"Don't get your hopes up," the old woman said grumpily. "We're only going as far as the campground so I can park my stuff with that Fred Allison. Then we've *got* to head for Hobart Street. This tub hasn't got enough gas left in it to get out to that Chiltern Place place and back."

"That's okay," Boo said quickly. "I've got—I've got fifteen dollars in my purse. Is that enough for gas?"

Auntie gave her a sharp look. "Sure. Ten oughta be enough." At the next stop light she said, "Tell you what. You give me three of what's left over, for a hamburger and fries and bus fare back down to the campground, and you've got a deal."

"Deal," Boo agreed. "And if you want to, you can leave your stuff locked up in Elvira until Daddy gets here."

The police were gone from Chiltern Place, but at the far end of the driveway of one house a wide yellow plastic ribbon printed with the warning POLICE BARRIER—DO NOT CROSS told Boo and Auntie that number 1010 must be the Dickery house. Parking around the corner in a patch of shade, they walked back to the driveway of 1010.

Auntie hung back, and even Boo felt suddenly timid. The house was like one out of the pages of a magazine or in a movie. The stone it was made of was cream colored, and its windows were tall and arched. Boo had never seen a house so big or so fancy, with such velvety grass and masses of flowers out front. The trees were tall with swoopy branches, or short with flowers all over. And the driveway was five times as long as the Smiths' old one on Hobart Street. *Six* times, maybe.

Boo started up it. A four-car garage—*four* cars?—sat at the far end, and the yellow barrier tape was fastened across the doorways of the two open stalls. In one, the tail end of a big silver car stuck out, as if whoever parked it had been in too much of a hurry to get it all the way in.

Auntie stopped a little way in from the street and looked around her uneasily, as if she expected a squad of police officers to come crashing out of the shrubbery. "Don't you go touching anything," she called nervously as Boo went on ahead.

Both the front and side doors of the Dickery house were double doors, and the handles had been fastened together with an odd-looking padlock with a yellow tag that said POLICE SEAL. At the rear of the house, a lawn with trees and stone benches and a fish pond stretched on back, past a swimming pool to a tennis court at the far end. But it was the garage Boo was interested in. Ms. Cooperman had said that was where they left the big silver car she saw the fake Dickerys drive off in, and there it still was. *Please* let there be a

118

clue, Boo thought. There had to be, unless . . .

Unless the fake Dickerys had kept up their act the whole time and Cisco never suspected anything was wrong. But he must have, Boo argued to herself, if they changed cars right there in the garage. On his dumb old TV detective shows, crooks were always changing cars so they couldn't be followed, so right here, in this very place, he ought to have put two and two together.

It was hard looking for clues when she didn't know what the clue was that she was looking for. Boo wished she had paid more attention to the TV detectives, instead of reading while Cisco watched. And the looking wasn't made any easier by the yellow tape with its DO NOT CROSS. How was she supposed to see into the car if she didn't cross the line?

How? Go around it.

If, that is, the police had forgotten the garage's side door. Boo had spied the door in the shadowy back corner and wondered whether they could have. Since they didn't have to go through it to get in, maybe . . . To reach it she pushed through a little side gate and made her way past a neat row of trash cans. She found no yellow tape, no yellow tag. The door's hinges were stiff, as if it was never used, but at the second push it creaked open.

The car doors were locked, and Boo was careful not to touch the doors or windows as she peered in. But there was nothing to see. Either the fake Dickerys were very, very neat, or the police had swept up everything like a vacuum cleaner. Maybe they did use a vacuum cleaner. Maybe one of the little hand ones like Mrs. Maldonado's. Boo turned to look at the walls and floor. She had never seen such a tidy garage.

In the stalls behind the two closed doors, a jeep and a long convertible sat in the shadows, but there weren't any clues there either. Both cars were so dusty that it was easy to see that they hadn't been touched in weeks. A door in the back wall opened into a tiny bathroom. The floor there was clean too, except for a sycamore leaf or two that had blown in from the open stalls.

There was nothing. No crumpled-up scrap of paper with the fake Dickerys' real name scribbled on it, or the getaway car's license number. No message scratched on the wall with a stone. No anything. Boo, disappointed and more frightened than ever, stood in the bathroom doorway and kicked at the leaves, not knowing what to do next.

Until she saw the tiny, shiny clue one leaf had hidden.

She pounced on it like a cat on a slithery lizard, as if it might flicker away. It was a miniature pin— no, two pins, pinned together. They had to be from Cisco's precious collection: the Pittsburgh Pirates pin, and the "Dragnet" badge he traded his extra Olympic Diving one for.

In the outer garage, Boo dropped to her hands and knees to ruffle wildly through the rest of the leaves, but found nothing more. Still, two clues! Boo ducked under the yellow tape—after all, it didn't say DO NOT CROSS on its back side— and raced down the driveway.

Auntie, who in such a neat, well-groomed neighborhood looked almost as dumpy and rumpled as ever, was fidgeting out at the end of the drive. Because she was talking to a man who stood, rake in hand, in the next-door shrubbery, it was a moment before she saw Boo coming. When she did, she gave the man a quick nod and, grabbing Boo's arm, pulled her on down the sidewalk toward the street corner.

"Where in blazes you been all this time? You didn't touch anything, did you? That gardener next door there, he says the cops who were here got some kind of emergency call and had to go off before the fingerprint guys came, but they'll be back. You didn't touch anything, did you?"

"No, no. Except—" Boo pulled free and danced ahead of Auntie along the sidewalk. "Except I found something. Under some leaves in the garage. Look!"

Auntie peered at the little pins on Boo's palm.

"What the heck are those? Toy badges? So what?" She hurried on, as fast as the too-tight white sandals would take her.

"They're Cisco's. He's got this whole collection

121

of them," Boo panted as they reached Elvira. She could hardly fit the key in the door lock, she was jiggling up and down so with excitement. Scrambling in, she reached across to unlock the driver's door.

"Don't you get it? The one's a pirate. From the Pittsburgh Pirates. That means Cisco figured out they were being hijacked. The other one means 'Call the cops.' It's a police badge. See? He was laying a trail."

Auntie gave a sarcastic *Humph!* as Elvira pulled away from the curb. "Oh, sure. And we're supposed to stop at every corner so you can scrootch around on the sidewalk, looking for some bitty little banana or penguin that's going to tell us 'Turn here'?"

Boo considered. Los Angeles was such a huge place that it did sound goofy. "Okay. I guess it does just mean 'Call the cops. We're being hijacked.' Maybe he thought Ms. Cooperman would find it?"

"Hah! She didn't need any clue to figure that out, or to tell her to call the cops." Auntie scowled. "Well, they've already been called. Great. We come all the way out here to find out what we already know.

"Keep your eye peeled for a gas station," she grumbled as the van turned onto Wilshire Boulevard.

* * *

122

Elvira had just turned off the Pasadena Freeway and was sailing up Avenue 43 toward Figueroa Street when Boo remembered the gardener on Chiltern Place.

"What were you and that man talking about? You know, that gardener."

Auntie shrugged. "Just about how the cops were in and out of the house and all over. They asked him and all the neighbors a lot of questions, too."

"Like what?"

"About how much time those kid-snatchers spent there, and what kind of car they had. A plum-colored van, he said. Seems they kept it shut up, but he saw it once: a plum-colored Dodge van with a big, funny-shaped dent on the passenger-side door. Looks like an elephant. Some joker even painted a trunk on it."

Boo sat up straight. "An elephant? A dent like an elephant? I've seen that. I've seen a van like that somewhere. I know I have!"

10

THE MORNING SUNSHINE THREADED ITS
way through the tall, dense hedge of redwood
trees across the Dockett driveway and sent flick-
ering bright fingers of light through the thin curtains of the upstairs windows. One touched
Poppy's eyelid for a moment and glittered in her
dream. She was dreaming about being in a boat
on the ocean. The boat was taking her out to
watch the whales and their babies swim and spout
in the sunshine and slap their beautiful tails on
the water, just like on TV.

The sunlight fluttered back across Poppy's face.
She lifted a sleepy hand to bat it away. When that
didn't work, she opened one eye.

And sat straight up in the top bunk with a gasp.
Whose bedroom was she *in?*

"Cisco? *Cisco!*"

Cisco turned over and buried his face in his
pillow. "Ummph-mmm . . . Whunh?"

Poppy quickly wiped her tears of relief on the

124

sheet so Cisco wouldn't see. It was all right if J.D. and Peachie thought she was still a baby, not just a shrimp. They didn't matter. Cisco did.

"It's okay," she whispered. "For a minute I couldn't remember where we were." It was a scary feeling.

Cisco pushed himself up to sit with his legs hanging over the edge. He gave a yawn and stretched his arms toward the ceiling. "We don't *know* where we are," he said. He frowned and rubbed his eyes.

"Wherever this house is, I don't like it," Poppy whispered unhappily. She peered over the edge of her bunk. Babba and Danny still had not stirred, so she kept her voice low. "This house is scary. Not spooky-scary, but, but . . . " She wasn't exactly sure what she did mean.

"It is kind of funny, I guess," Cisco said slowly. "It doesn't feel really *real.* Maybe it's just because everybody keeps so quiet most of the time."

"Then why's it scary now when nobody's up yet to keep quiet?" Poppy asked. It was a very Poppy sort of question, and because he had no answer, Cisco pretended he hadn't heard.

Instead, he looked across to the red plastic clock on the top shelf of the bookcase that stood near the window. There were no books in the bookcase, only stacks of boxes of jigsaw puzzles. That was almost the weirdest thing of all about the house: there was nothing to read. Cisco couldn't understand that. Even people who never learned to like books read magazines and newspapers, didn't they?

The red clock read five minutes past eight. Sunshine flickered in through the thin curtains and through the slats of the shutters across the bottom half of the window. He stared at the shutters, frowning, then suddenly swung himself down to the floor and padded to the door.

It opened easily.

"What's the matter?"

Cisco closed the door silently. "Nothing. I just had this weird dream," he said slowly. "I dreamed I woke up in the middle of the night and opened the window. But it's shut."

"That's not weird."

"What I saw out the window was. There was this black van, and it came creeping along the driveway without any lights on. Or any noise. And when it stopped, all these humpy shadows got out and swarmed around. Like animals."

Poppy shivered. "I hope they didn't come into the house."

"Don't be silly. It was only a dream," Cisco said. But he remembered that Poppy sometimes had dreams that frightened her, so he tried to think of something cheerful to talk about.

"I almost forgot!" He brightened. "That Ms. Cooperman's supposed to come at nine o'clock. I bet she'll say Mom's all okay and waiting for us

126

back at the campground. We'd better wake Babba and Danny and get dressed."

Poppy climbed down eagerly.

On most mornings Babba and Danny were hard to wake, and growled like sleepy little bears, but this time they sat up, wide awake, at the first sight of the strange room.

"Are we still at the Cookie Witch's house?" Babba asked in a small voice.

"Yes," Poppy answered. She dragged the desk chair across the carpet to the closet so that she could reach the clothes she had hung there the night before.

Danny stuck his lower lip out. "If that old Wolf Man tries to eat me, I'll bonk him on the nose. I will."

Cisco pulled the pajama top over Danny's head. "Sure you will. Even if he gives you ice cream for breakfast."

"*Will* he?" Danny's eyes widened.

Cisco didn't have a chance to answer, because just then Sugar stuck her head in at the door to give the four Smiths a sour look. "Breakfast in fifteen minutes," she announced, and then vanished as silently as she had come.

"Cisco," Poppy hissed. "Look! All our clothes are gone."

"Don't be silly," Cisco said. He wasn't really listening, but wondering how Sugar could always look so grumpy in a house so full of wonderful things. What could be neater than living in a house with a video recorder and a whole bookcase full of movie videos? It was too bad Ms. Cooperman was coming so early in the morning. He wouldn't get to see a single one.

Poppy stamped her foot. *"Cisco!"*

Cisco turned to see her still standing on the chair in the closet doorway. "I told you. See, they're gone."

And they were.

In their place hung four new-looking pairs of jeans and four blue-and-white-striped T-shirts exactly like the ones the other children had worn. Of their old things, only the tennis shoes were left.

"All righty," J.D. said. He took a big swig from his coffee cup. "Everybody dig in."

Each place at the long dining-room table was set for breakfast with a bowl of corn flakes, a glass of orange juice, and a knife and fork and spoon and plate and mug. The middle of the table was crowded with pitchers of milk, a thermos jug of coffee, butter dishes, one platter of scrambled eggs and bacon and another heaped with toast, and open jars of jam and honey. The Smith children stared at the feast and then at each other. They had never seen such a breakfast.

"C'mon! Dig in, kids. Cereal first." J.D. took a big spoonful himself.

"No, no! Napkins first," Peachie warned. She

reached for the sugar bowl and spooned a little over her cereal and a lot into her coffee. "But J.D.'s right, kiddies. You sit there like four little old bumps on a log, and this bunch'll gobble up all the eggs and bacon before you get to 'Pass the milk.' "

"That's for sure," J.D. said. He pushed his empty bowl aside and reached for the toast. "Eat up. I never did see such a skinny little thing as that pretty little Poppy. You could use some butter and jam and eggs and bacon, honey. But don't you worry. We'll get you fattened up real quick."

Babba stopped in the middle of reaching for her orange juice. Slipping down from her chair, she grabbed at Poppy's arm as Poppy poured milk over her cereal.

"No!" Babba shrieked. "Don't eat it. Don't get fat, Poppy!"

J.D. and Peachie and the seven other children stopped eating and stared.

Cisco felt his ears go fiery red.

"She's okay. She's just goofy in the head sometimes," he blurted. It would be awful if Peachie caught on about the oven and the Cookie Witch. Cisco got up to go pry Babba loose from Poppy, and gave her a shove back onto her chair.

"Go on, you silly goofus." He grinned, trying to turn it into a joke. "Hurry up and eat. We've got to finish before Ms. Cooperman comes. She said nine o'clock."

J.D. put down his piece of marmalade toast. Peachie's hands flew to her face.

"Oh dear, oh *dear*," she cried in a soft little wail. "And here I meant to tell you first thing."

"Tell us what?" Poppy and Cisco asked in the same quick breath.

"That nice Ms. Cooperman," J.D. explained. "She gave us a call just now before you came down. Said she couldn't make it before tomorrow. And you're not to fret about your momma. She's still in the hospital and doing just fine. Be out tomorrow or Saturday. So you'll be here for another day or two after all."

"And we'll have us such fun you won't have *time* to fret!" Peachie announced cheerfully.

"Let's play Snatch!" the Three Monkeys yelled.

"Now, that wouldn't be fair," Peachie said. "Not until the Smiths learn the rules. No. But eat up all your breakfast, and after J.D.'s gone off to work we'll have a game of Sneak. That's a good place to start, and we'll keep score. The one who improves the most gets to pick a video movie for after lunch. And second place gets to pick which flavor ice cream for dessert at lunch. How about that?"

Sneak? Poppy and Cisco looked at each other. What kind of game was that? But Poppy could see that what Cisco was really thinking of were the bookshelves full of movie videos.

Already cereal spoons all around the table were hard at work. A moment later Cisco's was too.

Even Poppy's. Only Danny's stayed on the table.

"I don' *like* corn flakes." Danny sulked.

"Not like *corn* flakes!" Peachie threw up her hands. "Well, then, we'll just have to find something else for you, sweetie, won't we?"

Popping out of her chair, Peachie swept up Danny's bowl and headed for the kitchen. A moment later she was back to plunk another down in front of him.

It was a bowl of chocolate ice cream.

"Hey!" Danny yelled, scrootching up to the edge of his chair. "Ice cream for brekfuss!" He grabbed for his spoon.

"Me too, please," Chuckie called. He held up his empty bowl.

Chuckie put his bowl down again in a hurry as J.D.'s bushy brows drew together in a wolfish scowl. The awful scowl was gone almost as soon as it appeared—so quickly that only Chuckie and Poppy, who had a pokey eater's wandering eye, saw it.

Poppy shivered, but made herself finish her cereal and orange juice. When Cisco passed the toast, she shook her head. "I don't want any, please," she whispered.

For Poppy, Friday and Ms. Cooperman couldn't come any too soon.

Up in the attic playroom, Sugar explained Sneak. To Poppy's relief the game wasn't about trying to sneak up on and scare the other players.

Cisco was disappointed that it wasn't some kind of spooky hide-and-seek. In a hiding game there would be chances to have a closer look at the video recorder in the living room and to explore more of the house than they had seen. He might even find out how to open the secret staircase hidden behind one of the living-room cupboards.

Instead, Sneak turned out to be a little bit like gym class and a lot like a bunch of little kids fooling around on the school playground. The difference was that the tasks and games were put together like an obstacle course. First came a knotted rope to swarm up, then the balance beam to walk on, the jungle gym to climb over or swing across monkey fashion, a set of stairs that went up and then right down again, and the fat, twisty plastic pipe for crawling through. A new player started as soon as the last one finished, and Peachie kept time. Poppy wondered why it was called Sneak, but was too shy to ask.

Peachie sat perched on a stool by a little table. The table held a pencil and paper, an odd-looking black metal box the size of a shoe box, and a timer clock with the stop button on top, like the ones used by chess players to time their moves. On the wall beside the table was a blackboard with a line drawn down the middle. At the top the words FIRST ROUND were lettered on the left-hand side and SECOND ROUND on the right.

" . . . only," Sugar finished with a smirk, "you

little ones don't have strong enough arms to climb ropes, so that part's just for George and me. And since I'm too big to wriggle through the pipe, I climb the rope again at the end. Everybody else starts at the balance beam and goes all the way around from there. Okay?"

Everyone said okay except George, a glum-looking boy with lank, brown hair who never seemed to say anything.

Cisco didn't like being lumped in with the younger children, but he didn't say so.

Poppy had to explain the game a second time to Babba and Danny. By the time Tina and Tim and the Three Monkeys had gone around, the younger Smiths knew just what to do. Babba was slow, but did everything perfectly. Danny slipped, tripped, slithered, and bumped, but was fast. Poppy herself forgot J.D. and Peachie and the shivers they gave her by the time she came to the jungle gym. She began to have fun. After all, her secret wish was to grow up to be a circus acrobat, and until school let out for the summer, she had practiced every day on the playground at recess. She was so light and fast that Sugar made a face like a lemon and stomped across to check the timer.

Cisco was last. Not to be outshone by Poppy, he decided to ignore Sugar's rule, and started as she and George had, by swarming up the knotted rope hand over hand and gripping the knots with

133

his feet. The rope was too near the wall and his feet kept banging against it, but he made it all the way up to the ceiling.

"Dear me," Poppy heard Peachie say to herself. "Surprise, surprise! That kid's got to be older'n eight."

When Cisco came wiggling out of the end of the wriggle tunnel, Peachie punched the stop button. Then she looked at the strip of paper that came out of the black box and wrote some numbers down in the score book.

"Well, well," she exclaimed. "Aren't you the fast one!"

Sugar looked grumpier than ever.

Poppy didn't care as much about the score as the fun, but Cisco held his breath. He was pretty sure both he and Poppy had been at least as fast as George even if George had played the game a lot. But Sugar was a lot bigger and stronger.

Peachie finished her adding up and, still very businesslike, crossed to the blackboard. On the left side, under the words FIRST ROUND, she wrote in the names and scores:

George	85
Poppy	76
Tina	75
Sugar	72
Tim	68
Sam	62

Chuckie	55
Harry	53
Babba	46
Cisco	40
Danny	40

Peachie switched her bright smile back on and twinkled happily at Poppy. "Seventy-six! The very first time, too! Why, J.D. is goin' to be thrilled to *pieces*."

Cisco stared. He couldn't believe it. He was tied for last with *Danny*?

"But—"

Peachie turned her twinkle on Cisco, and her laugh tinkled out. "Don't you worry, Francisco honey. Sugar there, she forgot to tell you one little old thing. Being quiet counts lots more than being fast."

Cisco looked baffled. "Quiet?"

"It's J.D.'s idea. To make the game harder, see?" Peachie moved back to the little table. "See this black box? This's what's called an audiometer. It measures sound and prints out these little squiggles on the paper tape. Loud noises—your feet bumping the wall—make big squiggles. See there?"

"We get to try again, don't we?" Cisco was suddenly cheerful. If the winner was going to be the player who improved the most, then being on the bottom had to be good luck.

The second time around everyone, even Danny, tried to be quiet as mice. Peachie's scoreboard showed the difference.

George	83
Poppy	78
Sugar	76
Tina	73
Cisco	72
Tim	70
Sam	60
Chuckie	56
Harry	55
Babba	55
Danny	52

"Hey!" Cisco crowed. "I went up thirty-two points. I win. I get to pick the movie!"

"Indeed you did, sweetie."

Cisco was too pleased with himself to see the smug, satisfied look Peachie gave him as she spoke, but Poppy did. It was a look that a cat which had caught a fat mouse might wear.

Or a Cookie Witch watching Hansel gobble up her cookies and cake and cream.

11

AS THE CHILDREN LINED UP TO GO downstairs, Peachie announced that after the after-lunch movie they would play a game of Seek. Not hide-and-seek; just "Seek."

"Don't you ever do anything besides play games and watch movies?" Poppy whispered to Tina. Tina shook her head and edged away a little, to stand close to her brother. Without Tina's longer blond curls and shyer manner, it would have been difficult to tell the twins apart even though they were not identical.

Tim was almost as shy, but not quite. "We don't even have to go to school," he whispered.

Cisco thought that sounded even more exciting than having a thirty-six-inch TV screen.

Poppy said it was a fib and she didn't believe one word.

Certainly not everything in the Dockett house was play and games. Poppy found herself a

137

Peachie's Helper at lunchtime, along with Tim. Tim showed her how Peachie liked the table set, and when that was done they carried in the pitchers of lemonade and bowls of salad with apples and raisins. The big bowl of Spanish rice, with lots of sausage bits in it, was heavy and hot, so Peachie carried that. Poppy, who loved sausage, ate so much that she surprised herself. When time for dessert came, she was too full to eat any, even though Danny picked butterscotch ripple, her favorite.

Danny was in seventh heaven. Maybe eighth. To his delight, and Babba's, Peachie didn't send them upstairs afterward for naps. At home, and even at the campground, they always had to take an hour's nap after lunch, like babies. Peachie, once her helpers had fitted all of the dishes in the dishwasher, shooed all eleven children into the living room, switched on the VCR, slid in the cassette Cisco had chosen, and bustled out again, shutting the door behind her.

Cisco's choice, after twenty minutes of dithering back and forth along the shelves of movie cassettes before lunch, had finally been *The Mark of Zorro.* Even Poppy—to her own surprise— enjoyed it. It was fun to see the hero fool the villains by pretending to be a wimp, but best of all were the horses. It would be wonderful, Poppy thought, to crouch low over a horse's neck and ride like the rushing wind over the hills and down through the shadowy woods. . . .

Halfway through the movie, it turned out that Peachie's no-naps idea was pretty sneaky. Babba and Danny and the Three Monkeys, curled up on the two sofas, dropped off to sleep one by one. They woke only when, just before the end, Peachie opened the door at the far end of the living room and pushed in a little table on wheels, with fruit punch in paper cups and two big bowls of popcorn.

By the time "THE END" flashed on the screen, the cups were empty and the popcorn gone. Peachie showed Cisco how to make the video player spit the movie cassette back out, and while he fitted the tape into its box and returned it to the shelf, she began to collect the paper cups. Babba helped. Danny climbed down from the sofa too, and had to be stopped from pushing all the video buttons. The other children sat still, as if they were waiting for an announcement.

"I bet she claps her hands," Poppy whispered in Cisco's ear.

Cisco frowned, but the very next minute Peachie did clap her hands. "Listen up, kiddies!" she said. "We still have time for that game of Seek before J.D. gets home from work. How about it?"

Tim and the Monkeys cheered. Even Sugar seemed pleased as she went to a cupboard and brought out a small tin box. Only George didn't crack a smile; the way he squinted up his eyes and jiggled his heels on the floor made it hard to tell whether he was excited or anxious.

Poppy turned to whisper to Cisco. "What kind of work do you s'pose J.D. goes to?"

Cisco shrugged. He was busy wondering how much VCRs cost and how long it would take to save up for one.

Poppy frowned. "Do you s'pose their kids don't *really* do anything but play?"

Cisco gave her the look of good-humored scorn he usually used on Babba. "Don't be silly. She was just pulling your leg."

Peachie had very sharp ears. "Oh, no," she twittered cheerily. "That is pretty near all. What better way to spend a day?"

With a flourish, she tipped the contents of the little tin box out onto the coffee table. They were shiny colored buttons with pins on the back. Peachie handed one to each of the children: green, yellow, and purple to the Three Monkeys, white and orange to Tina and Tim, and gold to Sugar. George made a face when he got the brown badge, but not until he saw Peachie wasn't looking. Babba's, to her delight, was the pink one. Pink was the color she liked best of all, just as Danny, who got the red badge, liked red best. Cisco ended up with the blue one, and Poppy the silver, which was really weird. Peachie, Poppy thought with a shiver, must be a mind reader. How else could she have picked each of the Smith children's favorite colors?

Seek-the-Treasure—Seek for short—was nothing like any treasure hunt Cisco and Poppy had played before. Players had to look for objects bearing stickers of the same color as their badges: at least two for the older children, and one apiece for the little ones. Peachie gave each child a cloth bag like a small pillowcase to put the "treasures" in. And there were to be prizes for everyone, but the best prize would go to the fastest player. Except for J.D.'s office, no room in the house was off limits. Not even Peachie and J.D.'s bedroom.

Cisco's smile widened as the rules were explained, but it vanished at the very last one: the game was to start outside the house. With all the doors locked.

Peachie took Danny and Babba by the hand and explained once again about finding their red and pink stickers, and then went to the side door to count heads as the children crowded out past her and down the steps. They lined up quietly along the driveway.

"Remember," Peachie warned. "Look in places where you might *really* find something valuable. Ready? Steady. Go!" On the word *Go* she shut the door with a bang. There was a loud *snick!* as the lock snapped shut.

The other children shot off in all directions, leaving the Smiths standing in the middle of the driveway. Sugar vanished around the back of the house. George clambered up one of the vine-covered pillars of the carporch outside the side door and crossed its roof to an open bedroom window. Chuckie, the smallest of the Monkeys, darted back up the steps and wriggled in through a pet door the Smiths had not noticed before. The other two small boys worked at prying open a cellar window, while Tina, and then Tim, climbed the morning-glory trellis on the side of the house and vanished through another bedroom window.

Cisco gave Danny a shove toward the pet door. "Go on! Follow Chuckie. You too, Babba." As they obediently scrambled up the steps, he ran for the trellis.

Poppy hesitated for a moment, then made a dash for the nearest car-porch pillar.

Inside the house it was hard to tell there was a game going on at all. Small feet pattered quietly upstairs and around and down and back and forth, and none of the players—except Danny, who couldn't help it—yelled or even laughed when they found their sticker on a "treasure."

Sugar, who had picked the lock on the back door to get into the house, finished first. She found her gold-colored stickers on the radio alarm clocks in her own room and J.D. and Peachie's. Cisco came in second, but only because the first place he looked was in the living room, and there were blue stickers on six of the newest-looking video cassettes. Babba found a pink one on the smaller of the two jewel boxes on Peachie's dressing table, and Danny's red one turned up on the little bathroom scale that said *"Your-weight-is-thirty-pounds-and-twelve-ounces"* when he stood on it. Poppy's silver-colored sticker, stuck on the rim of the open silverware drawer in the dining-room cupboard, was almost too easy to find. A little arrow pointed to the silver spoons. If she had scurried, she could have beaten Sugar for first place in spite of Sugar's head start.

Instead Poppy came trailing in next-to-last.

Peachie was waiting in the living room with her timer. She gave Poppy a sharp look, but quickly switched on a bright smile. "Thirty-seven minutes! Now, that's not at all bad, kiddies. Not with four beginners playing and a whole house to search. We'll have us another hunt as soon as everything's back in place and I've put out more stickers. I just bet you'll do lots better. But right now it's time for this hunt's prizes, right?"

"Right!" everyone cried at once.

To Cisco and Poppy's astonishment, and Babba and Danny's delight, when Peachie went to unlock the cupboard next to the videotape shelves, they saw that it held eleven big, fat glass jars. Each had a slot cut in the lid and a white name sticker on the front, and several were full almost to the top with coins, mostly dimes and quarters. Four empty jars labeled FRANCISCO, POPPY, BARBARA, and DANNY stood on the lower shelf.

The Seek prizes were money! Not choosing videos, or ice-cream flavors for dessert, but real honest-to-goodness money. Sugar's jar was only the second fullest, but a lot of the coins were like the funny-looking ones that showed here and there in the other jars. They had a woman's face on them, and the lettering underneath said ONE DOLLAR. None of the Smith children had ever seen a dollar coin before.

Babba's eyes widened, and her mouth made a little round *O* of delight as Peachie counted out five dimes into her hand for being seventh in the hunt. Babba liked nickels and dimes even more than Danny liked double chocolate ice cream.

"No, not in your pocket, you silly!" Peachie gave her a tweak on the cheek. "You're s'posed to put 'em in your own special jar. See? This one has your name on it: B-A-R-B-A-R-A. Barbara."

Poppy found she had won four nickels. Cisco got ten dimes, and Danny two nickels. Everyone won something.

"There!" Peachie said as the last nickel went *tink!* into its jar. "And when your jar's full up, we'll change all the nickels and dimes and quarters for dollars so you'll have room to put still more in."

On the way upstairs to get cleaned up for supper, Cisco squinted. How many dimes would it take to buy his own video recorder-player to take back to Pittsburgh, if a VCR cost two hundred dollars?

Babba, ahead of him, turned at the top of the steps. "*I'm* going to get a dollar," she announced smugly. "Peachie said so. But I can't tell. 'Sa secret."

"Me too," said Danny.

"Everybody gets a whole dollar every time we play Snatch," came Tina's faint whisper in Poppy's ear.

But Poppy barely heard. She was too frightened. Why, if Ms. Cooperman was coming in the morning to take them back to their mother, had Peachie put their names on four new money jars? Four *big* new money jars.

Worst of all was what she had said. . . .

"When your jar's full up."

Full up. That would take months. *Years.*

12

THE HOT CHOCOLATE THAT PEACHIE brought up on a tray at bedtime was delicious even if it was a funny sort of treat for summertime. She gave the green mugs to Cisco and Poppy and the pretty blue ones to Babba and Danny. "Don't you tell the other kids," she whispered as if they were all in a plot together. "This is special just for you four, since it's maybe your last night here. Drink up now, so's I can take the mugs back downstairs with me."

Maybe it was the hot chocolate but, worry or no, Poppy was asleep in no time. Cisco, after punching his pillow a time or two, soon drifted off too. Babba and Danny took longer. They muttered and twitched like puppies dreaming of exciting chases and juicy bones, but Cisco and Poppy never stirred.

At least, not for a long while.

The glow-in-the-dark hands on the little red

clock on the bookcase were at the two and the
three when something—a movement? a sound?—
made Poppy stir and then sit up. She sat blinking
for a long moment before she was truly awake.
Even then she didn't know why she was awake.
The bedroom was only faintly lit by moonlight,
and the house was so quiet that her own breathing
seemed loud. Cisco lay sprawled on the other top
bunk, deep in sleep. Poppy leaned over the edge
of her bunk to peer at Babba. Babba, who always
slept curled up, looked strangely stiff and straight
under her sheet.

"Babba? Are you okay?" Poppy hissed. When
Babba didn't stir, Poppy slid down the ladder in
a rush.

"*Babba!*" Frightened, she gave the sheet a sharp
tug.

Two pillows lay there. No Babba.

Two more were neatly covered by Danny's
sheet. He was gone too.

"Cisco!" Poppy shrieked, but as softly as she
could, so that no one else would hear. When Cisco
did not stir, she climbed part way up his bunk
ladder and jiggled his leg.

"Cisco? *Please* wake up," she wailed.

But Cisco only groaned and stretched and
turned to face the wall.

Poppy punched his leg. Hard. Then, desper-
ate, she climbed up another rung, leaned over,
and bit him on the ankle.

"Arr-OW-W!" Cisco sat up with a sleepy roar and blinked at Poppy's dark shape. "Whoozat? Somebody *bit* me!" He hugged his foot to him.

"It's me. Poppy. I had to. You wouldn't wake up," she whispered frantically. "Babba and Danny are gone. What'll we do?"

"Gone?" Cisco mumbled stupidly. He was only half awake. "What do you mean, 'gone'?"

"*Gone*-gone," Poppy hissed.

"For Pete's sake," Cisco grumbled. "They probably went to the bathroom. Maybe Danny was scared to go by himself."

"But somebody fixed pillows under their sheets to look like they're still there." Poppy pulled at his pajama leg. "Come on. *Look.*"

Cisco was suddenly very much awake. Nobody fixed pillows under sheets just to go to the bathroom. In a moment he was down the ladder and at the door.

The door handle would not turn.

"It's locked. Like in that nutty dream I had last night." Cisco stared at the door handle and then at his sister. "Only it *wasn't* a dream. Unless this is." Fat chance. His ankle still smarted from Poppy's bite, and he felt as awake as he was frightened.

Poppy shook her head, and then froze with a warning finger at her lips.

The window's bottom sash was open only a crack, but from somewhere not far away a faint mechanical whine floated up through the night air and in through the window and the shutters' slats. In a moment Cisco had eased the sash up far enough to stick his head out. Poppy, remembering his tale of strange, dark figures and a shadowy van, leaned out too.

The noise had been the gate closing. As the children watched, the dark bulk of the van came purring into view, headlights switched off, from under the car porch and rolled to a stop in front of the garage. What had seemed so eerie the night before when Cisco was half asleep seemed odder still when he wasn't. The rear doors swung open and five small, dark figures, hand in hand, scurried out of sight around the back of the house. The van crept on into the garage, where a dim light flicked on and taller shadows moved busily to and fro.

"Ssst! They're coming!" Poppy dashed for the ladder and in a moment was under her sheet, with her face to the wall.

Cisco was almost as fast, but he lay facing the door and burrowed his head into his pillow just far enough so that he could still watch the doorknob out of the corner of one slitted eye.

If he hadn't been watching, he would never have known a door could open so silently. Poppy never heard a thing, and there was only a tiny jiggle of the bed and faint rustle of pillows and sheets to tell her that Babba had climbed back

into the lower bunk. It was several moments before Cisco reached over to give her an "all-clear"
nudge.

As soon as their feet touched the floor, it was
Babba they headed for. Babba the Blabber.

"Where *were* you?" they hissed in the same
breath.

"I'm asleep," Babba mumbled into her sheet.

"You are not."

"I am," came the small, stubborn voice.
"Peachie said so."

"Okay," Cisco said softly. "But if you don't wake
up this minute, you're going to get a fox bite."
He took hold of a soft part of her arm between
his thumb and fingers, ready for the twisty pinch
Boo used when she was feeling really mean. It
hurt like anything, so it was a good thing Boo
hardly ever felt that mean.

No one had ever fox-bitten Babba. She sat up
in alarm.

"Where were you?" Poppy repeated.

"I dunno." Babba's eyes were wide and inno-
cent. "Somewheres."

"Grr-r-r," Cisco growled and pretended to
tighten his pinch.

Babba loved secrets almost as much as she loved
being fussed over, but Danny was better at keeping them. Still, at Peachie's urging she had both
crossed her heart and hoped to die before she
told, *and* locked her lips and thrown away the

150

key. All that afternoon after they played Seek she had itched to tell Poppy about Peachie's promise of a shiny new silver dollar for keeping the secret. But she had kept quiet. Now the dollar was safely in her own money jar.

"We played Snatch," Babba whispered in a happy rush. "Peachie took us. Just us and Chuckie and Harry and Sam. We played Snatch over at Mr. and Mrs. Brown's house, and I won a silver dollar and Danny won one too. And I won this!" She opened one small, plump hand.

In her palm lay Peachie's tiny shiny heart-shaped locket on its thin glittery chain.

"I won it 'cause I found the jool box," Babba said proudly. And then, having let the cat out of the bag, she remembered her promise to Peachie and refused to say another word.

13

"I DON'T CARE WHAT YOU SAY," SUGAR said huffily. "I don't see why *I* couldn't have gone."

"That'll be enough of that," J.D. snapped. "You eat your breakfast and mind how you talk to your mother."

"Fair's fair," Peachie said. "If I took you, I'd have had to take Tim and Tina and George and Francisco and Poppy, and the Browns only invited the little ones. They said that little ones were too young to be any good at Snatch, so I made them a bet that our little ones could be as quiet as kittens. And we won! Besides," she said slyly, "there's no need for the rest of you to sulk. We're invited over to the Baxters' tonight. Regular prizes for Snatch *and* a special one from the Baxters. If we finish without getting caught, they'll treat us all to a trip to Disneyland."

Danny's eyes grew round as quarters. "Where Mickey Mouse lives?"

"That's right," J.D. said. "And Minnie and Goofy and Donald."

Babba jiggled up and down on her chair, fizzy with excitement. Silver-dollars-and-gold-lockets-and-Sleeping-Beauty's-castle-and-Tinker-Bell-and . . . and . . . It was all wonderful. She slipped down from her chair and ran to throw her arms around Peachie's neck and give her a smoochy, orange-juicy kiss.

"Don't!" Peachie pulled away sharply and rubbed at her cheek. A second later she was smiling her sparkly smile again. She patted Babba on her head. "My little lambie," she cooed, and then patted her own head to make sure her topknot curls were not mussed.

"You, Sugar," she said, "can help keep score tonight. J.D.'s got a full day's work to put in, so he'll be too tired to go."

Cisco smothered a grin. With Sugar out of the game, he would have a good chance to come in first in the treasure hunt, or at least second, after George.

Poppy wasn't interested in the game. "Isn't Ms. Cooperman coming this morning?" she asked timidly as soon as everyone else was busy eating.

Cisco felt his face go red. He had forgotten all about Ms. Cooperman. J.D. turned his bushy-browed look on Poppy, and even though a friendly smile went with it, his pale eyes made her want to shiver.

153

"That's what she said, pretty Poppy: 'Friday, or Saturday at the latest.' So if she doesn't turn up today, she'll be here tomorrow for sure."

"Good," Poppy said in a very small voice.

Friday, like Thursday, went by with Sneak and Seek and no Ms. Cooperman. The afternoon video was a Three Stooges movie, Sam's choice. Dinner was spaghetti with lots of sauce, and a salad with cheese in it, and banana ice cream with marshmallow sauce. Bedtime came early, at seven-thirty. "Snatch isn't fun if it isn't in the dark," Peachie explained. "But you can't be good at it if you're sleepy, so the rule is 'Get a good snooze in first.' "

Poppy had never played a game in the dark, and unlike Babba she was not made brave by the thought of silver dollars. It took her so long to get to sleep that the snooze did not help, either. Then, when it was time to wake up and go, it was Sugar who came in to shake the Smiths awake. Her pale, sour face hanging over the bed in the darkness was so witch-spooky that Poppy nearly squeaked in fright.

Cisco and Babba were already up, but Danny, even after he sat up, was only half awake. He climbed out of bed when Babba tugged at his hand and stumped sleepily downstairs after her.

Sugar led the way to the dining room. The others were already there. The Three Monkeys sat lined up on chairs with their feet stuck out for J.D. and Peachie to pull dark socks on over their tennis shoes. They were quiet as mice, but their eyes were excited and their feet fidgety.

"Hello, look who's here! Four more sleepyheads," J.D. rumbled.

"You got their clothes, Sugar?" Peachie asked.

Sugar had. At least she had four pairs of jeans over one arm and four pairs of tennis shoes dangling by their laces.

"That's the ticket," J.D. said. He took the shortest pair of jeans and, lifting Danny onto his lap, pulled them on over the striped pajama bottoms. After the jeans came a dark blue sweat shirt over the pajama tops, then the tennis shoes with the dark socks on the outside.

Danny, awake at last, frowned at his feet. "That's silly. My feet are inside out again."

"That's so your shoes won't squeak on the floor and spoil the game. Remember?" J.D. explained. But just at that moment Danny, no longer sleepy, noticed whose lap he was on, and whose hairy wolf-man hands were pulling up his socks.

"Lemme down!" Yelling, he wriggled free. "Lemme down!"

"Hush-shh-shh!"

As quick as magic, Peachie was at Danny's side with a bag of chocolate caramels. "One apiece for now," she whispered. "And two in your pocket for later." Danny took four because he wasn't very good at counting, and then Peachie offered the bag to the others, who each took three.

155

"Now, everybody listen up," Peachie said. "'Specially Cisco and Poppy. Our kids have played Snatch lots of times, and Danny and Barbara once, so they know it's almost exactly the same as the way we play Seek—except it's more fun when you play it away from home. Now, Mr. and Mrs. Baxter are 'It,' but they don't know for sure when we're coming, and we don't want them to hear one single bump or sniffle until the game is over. Sugar'll put this sign on their bedroom door so you'll know which room to stay out of." Peachie held up a card with the word IT lettered on it.

J.D. looked around the circle of children, checking shoes and socks. "Okay. Hoods up!"

Even J.D., who wasn't going along, wore a dark, hooded sweatshirt—the summer night was cool—but his socks were inside his shoes. The hood tied around his face made his sandy red eyebrows look even bushier and his big nose even longer. All he needed were pointy ears and a long, furry tail. Babba giggled, and in a moment the others were giggling too, even Poppy. J.D. himself gave a rumbly "Har-har" of a chuckle.

"Okay, everybody quiet!" Peachie's sharp whisper cut the giggles short. She pointed at the door. "Go see if the coast is clear, Sugar, sweetie."

The back hall was dark and empty and the house silent.

"Here we go, then, sneak, seek, snatch!" Peachie trilled. "Quiet as shadows, now!"

156

"Good luck!" J.D. called after them.

Peachie drove very carefully, probably because there were a lot of corners to turn. The trip seemed to take a long time, but might have been no longer than half an hour. The Baxters' house sat in the middle of a large garden shaded from the moonlight by tall trees and surrounded by a low, thick hedge. At the back, a high brick wall faced the alley where Peachie parked the van. The children were all awake as she switched off the motor. They were too excited to be sleepy.

Peachie made a sign to Sugar, who reached under the front passenger seat and pulled out a bundle, which she passed back to George. George held a finger to his lips, then unrolled the bundle and gave to each of the children a dark cloth bag. Babba, feeling important, showed Poppy how to open and close the drawstring.

"They're for our treasures," Chuckie whispered.

"No talking, Monkey," warned Peachie in a sharp whisper. "And remember, little shadows look for little treasures. Even if you find a wonderful big one, it's a no-no-touch. Big ones are too heavy, and if you drop anything, we lose the game. Okay? Okay!"

She slid the side door of the van open carefully, so that it made hardly any sound at all. "Follow the leader," she whispered.

One large, two medium, and nine small shadows slipped out of the alley and around the corner to slide into the side garden through a thin spot in the low hedge. Sugar held back the stiff branches for the little ones and then followed at the end of the line. Peachie, the tall shape at the head of the line, kept to the shadows at the edge of the moonlit lawn and every once in a while stopped still as a statue to listen. At the edge of a paved area at the back of the house she held up a warning hand. Everyone stopped.

Peachie slipped across the moonlit pavement and knelt by the back door. The door had a dog door in it, and after fiddling at it for a moment with something she took from her pocket, she had it open. She turned and beckoned.

The Three Monkeys pattered quickly across the patio, to wriggle out of sight through the dog door. Babba and Danny followed, but at the last minute Danny held back.

"I don't like that hole. It's *dark* inside," he objected.

If Vulpo the Wolf Man had been there to say "Go!" he would have skittered right in. Peachie coaxed in a whisper and wheedled, then began to be angry—at least, she held his arm so tightly that it hurt, and her whisper sharpened to a hiss. "All right, then. Stay here with me. But no silver dollar, and no ice cream tomorrow."

"If I find lots of treasures, can I have Danny's dollar?" Babba whispered eagerly.

"No, you *can't*." Danny hit out at his sister and,

twisting away from Peachie's grasp, vanished through the little door and left its flap swinging behind him.

Babba followed.

Inside the house, moonlight almost as bright as lamplight poured through the tall windows and spilled across the floors. Stepping into the back hallway after two of the Monkeys had brought a chair to the door and undone all of the locks, Cisco and Poppy felt as if they had stepped into a movie. They had never seen such a house. The rooms were so big, and the curtains so silky and the carpets so soft! It was easy to be quiet. Even the stairs were carpeted. From the front hallway Chuckie, Sam, and Harry set off to explore the downstairs rooms. Babba, with Danny at her heels, headed for the wide stairway—and the bedrooms, Cisco supposed. If the Baxters' house was anything like Peachie and J.D.'s, that was where the jewelry-box treasures would be. He hoped she would remember the *IT* sign. She would scream bloody murder if she got in the wrong room and Mr. and Mrs. Baxter sat up in bed and yelled "Gotcha!"

Sugar, slipping back down the stairs after putting up the sign, waved her arms as if to say "Stop staring and get moving!" Cisco shook himself like a puppy coming out of a bath and set off in search of the living room.

Poppy turned in at the nearest door to escape

Sugar's scowl and found herself in a high-ceilinged dining room bright with the moonlight that fell through the tall windows. A chandelier covered with glittery crystals hung above the long dining table. The table was bare, but in the cupboard at one end of the buffet along the wall were two tall candelabra with holders for four candles on each. The cupboard at the other end held two more candlesticks and a silver coffeepot and pitcher and sugar bowl with curlicue handles on a silver tray. Poppy pulled open the topmost of the drawers in the middle and, under a soft, dark cloth, found dozens of heavy silver knives and forks and spoons.

She hesitated, then began to put spoons in her bag: one, two, three . . . Then with a shiver she shut the drawer and looked around unhappily. Something was wrong. The house felt—empty. That was it. It smelled empty, as if it had been shut up for days.

And Snatch?

Snatch . . .

Snatch wasn't a game at all. She was sure of it. J.D. and Peachie didn't know the Baxters. Snatch was . . . was . . .

Poppy turned and flew from the room in search of Cisco.

"Burgling?" Cisco, hugging a VCR to his chest, goggled at his sister. "You're nuts. Nobody's *tak-*

ing anything. I took a bagful of movie videos out to the back hall already, and as soon as Peachie wrote it down, Sugar put them in a pile right there so the Baxters'll find it when they come down to breakfast."

"But they're not here. Nobody's here."

"That's crazy," he objected. "Okay—Okay, I'll believe it if you go up and look in the bedroom that says *IT*. I dare you."

Poppy wavered. And then it was too late. Sugar was in the doorway, beckoning. Two minutes later the back door was closed on the heap of treasures in the hall, and the last of the children was out of the house and running for the shadows of the trees that edged the lawn.

14

BACK AT THE DOCKETT HOUSE, WHEN everyone was supposed to be asleep, Peachie's lessons in supersneakery came in handy again. Poppy settled down cross-legged on the floor with her ear to the four Smiths' bedroom door, and Cisco slipped out over the windowsill and down the trellis with only a faint rustle of morning-glory leaves.

Burglars! The word rang over and over again in Cisco's head as he made his way down the side of the house. Poppy said they were all *burglars*, that Peachie had taken them out burgling! It wasn't true, Cisco told himself for the tenth time. Why *couldn't* it really be a game Peachie had arranged with the Baxters? Maybe sneaking into someone's house in the dark on a bet that you wouldn't get caught was a bit nutty. So was bringing "treasures" down to Peachie so she could keep score on which players were best and fastest. But they *had* left everything right there, in the middle of the hall. The Baxters, when they came down to breakfast, would see they had lost the bet. It all sounded weird, but then J.D. and Peachie *were* pretty weird. Except maybe for their great TV set and the VCR and all the videos. Oh, please, Cisco thought as he reached the ground, don't let Poppy be right. Don't let playing Snatch mean going out burgling! The very word *burgle* had a nasty, gurglish sound that made him shiver.

But Cisco had to know. And know *how.* And the first thing a detective did was look for clues. Ms. Cooperman was coming in the morning. If he and Poppy were going to tell her that eleven kids had gone out on a burgling expedition, they needed proof. But even if he found some, the idea was so nutty that tidy, by-the-rules Ms. Cooperman probably wouldn't believe a word of it. Cisco could almost hear J.D. giving his deep guffaw and Peachie clapping her hands and giggling, and both of them catching their breath and saying wasn't it wonderful what imaginations children have?

The shadows were deep under the tall redwood trees across the driveway. Cisco moved one cautious step at a time, taking care not to rustle the needles on the ground or crunch a twig. The garage door was open, but he had to cross a patch of moonlight to reach it. He hesitated by the old green van parked just off the driveway. If the garage door was open, didn't that mean there was nothing inside to hide? The dark upstairs windows of the big, old house stared down at him. At least J.D. and Peachie's window, and Sugar's, were around at the front of the house. George and the Three Monkeys' was the nearest, and it *looked* blank. But if George was still awake and watching, he was smart enough to stand well back from the window.

Cisco took a deep breath and crossed the patch of moonlight in three swift strides.

Inside the garage the shadows were so deep that, once past the rear end of the plum-colored van, Cisco found he might as well be blindfolded. His hands touched one of the van's windows, but even as his eyes grew used to the darkness, he could not see inside.

But when he tried the side door handle, the door opened.

Nobody was going to leave bags full of clocks and silverware and stuff in an open van in an open garage. Cisco gave a soft whistle of relief as he felt around inside and found nothing. The "treasures" *were* all back at the Baxters'.

Unless—

There was still J.D. And the old, green van. Cisco's heart sank. *The old green van had still been warm where he leaned against the front end.* So, what if J.D. had been at the Baxters' all along? What if he had scooped up the loot from the hallway and driven home by the shortest way so that he

164

would get there before Peachie and the plum-colored van? J.D. could have unloaded and hidden the loot once the children were back inside the house. But where? Cisco touched the partition that divided the plum-colored van's stall from the other half of the garage, and knew the answer almost before he asked himself the question.

There was, he remembered, a big, fat padlock on the outer door of the closed stall. He moved along to the inner door, but it was locked too. Still, the partition did reach only to the rafters, not all the way to the roof. . . .

Cisco stood for a moment in the narrow space between the van and the partition and tried to see the garage in his mind just as it had looked on the afternoon he and Poppy and Babba and Danny had arrived. That was only days ago, but it felt like weeks.

Next to the door, he remembered, a coil of rope and a—a bamboo rake hung from nails. In the back corner were shelves that looked strong enough to be climbed like a ladder if they were empty. But they had been crowded with a jumble of old cans of paint and rusty tools and a lot of other garage-shelf junk that would rattle and clank if anyone so much as breathed on it.

That left—what?

The van. It left the van. The plum-colored van might be newer and fancier than Elvira, but the

165

shape was pretty much the same. And he had climbed on top of Elvira lots of times. Well, a couple of times. Like on New Year's, when they went to Pasadena early and camped out overnight to get a good parking place for the Rose Parade. Elvira was so close to Colorado Boulevard that Mr. Smith said the view from her roof was as good as from the fifty-dollar grandstand seats.

Cisco felt his way past the door in the partition to the coil of rope that hung on the wall, and slung the rope over his shoulder. He could use it for getting down on the other side. Then he felt his way back to the rear end of the van. From the rear bumper up to the rear door handle was a long stretch of a step for anyone as short as Cisco, but the narrow little rim above the door that was there to keep the rain out gave him a fingertip hold. That helped. In a moment he found himself on the roof. Peering into the darkness above, he found his eyes growing more used to the shadowy blackness. He could see a strip of faintly lighter shadow that might be a rafter. He stood, gingerly, and raised an arm to feel for it.

Even in the dark, getting onto the top of the partition was simple with the van so close to it, the rafter to hold onto, and two days' practice at climbing and swinging. Once he was up, Cisco looped the coil of rope over his arm, felt for one free end, wrapped it twice around the rafter, and tied a rolling hitch, a knot he had learned from his father's old *Boy Scout Handbook* and the strongest one he knew. Then, starting with the other end, he lowered the rest of the rope down the far side of the partition. He felt the end touch the floor just as he uncoiled the last loop.

Taking a deep breath, Cisco gripped the rope in both hands, turned, felt backward with one foot and, remembering Peachie's warning that silence was half the score, walked himself noiselessly down the wall. Just in time he remembered there might be a light switch, and got past without stepping on it. Near the bottom, his foot brushed against what turned out to be a cardboard carton, but that was a very small sound. Two points off, he decided, feeling proud of himself.

The trouble was, he couldn't see a thing and couldn't turn the lights on. The dim glimmer of moonlight shining through the frosted glass of the small window in the far garage wall was no help. It was barely enough to tell him where the outer wall was. He reached out to find the carton he had bumped and found its flaps sealed with plastic tape. Holding out his arms and feeling his way forward with one foot, he moved away from the wall. One hand touched something hard and cloth-covered.

Something hard, smooth under the cloth, squarish and flattish. With buttons and a slot along one side. It was sitting on top of—

Cisco's hands froze where they were as a light

sprang on in the other half of the garage.

Soft footsteps moved along close to the wall. Between the van and the wall.

Cisco didn't know whether to be more frightened of discovery or astonished at what he saw in the light that spilled over the top of the partition.

He had his hands on a VCR in a dark, cloth bag—the very one, he was sure, that he had snatched from the living room at the Baxters' (if that was their name). Worse, it was only the topmost of a stack of VCRs. Beside it was an even higher stack of compact-disk players. An open carton nearby was filled higgledy-piggledy with movie videos. The shelves along the back wall were crammed with toaster ovens and portable TVs and fancy coffee machines. There was a carton filled to overflowing with nothing but silver trays. Another held silver coffeepots and teapots. Microwave ovens and bigger TVs and tape decks were stacked everywhere. There had to be more electronic equipment in the Docketts' garage than in the big Circuit Circus store that advertised on TV. Cisco felt like Ali Baba, trapped in the treasure cave by the forty thieves.

Trapped by the chief thief, anyway. At least, it sounded as if there were only the one of him. J.D. No prowler would turn the lights on or be so careless about making noise.

The door handle rattled, and then was still. A

moment later the lights winked off and the footsteps moved out along the partition wall and away.

Cisco took a step backward so that he could lean against the wall. He let out a long, shaky breath and then began to feel along the partition. One hand brushed against the rope and he clutched at it but made no move to climb back up. It would be safer to wait ten minutes. Twenty, maybe. One close call a night was enough.

Poppy was having itches and twitches all over from the suspense. What was Cisco *doing*? Why wasn't he back yet? The temptation to dart across to the window for a quick look out at the garage was almost too much for her. But she stayed at her post, her ear pressed against the door panel.

If it hadn't been, she would never have heard the soft rub of metal against metal as the doorknob began to turn. The movement was so slight that she saw it only because it was right in front of her nose.

In a flash Poppy was up the bunk ladder once more and slipping between the sheets. The bed springs went *skreak!*, but that was OK. She pretended to shift drowsily, and then sat up as if she had been startled awake. Funnily enough, she didn't feel the least bit quivery or cowardy. Perhaps when you were playacting you felt so much like what you were pretending to feel that the quivers got sidetracked. She scrunched her eyes up to peer sleepily across at the other top bunk and the sheeted pillows that made such a convincing Cisco.

"Cisco? 'Zat you?"

When no answer came, she turned her head to look toward the door and made her eyes grow round at the sight of its widening crack. That was easy, because it *was* scary. She gave a little squeak of alarm, and then reached out to jiggle Cisco's make-believe foot.

"*Cisco!* The door!" she hissed.

"Uhn-nh," she answered herself with a low Cisco-ish snort.

As she watched, the door eased shut as silently as it had opened.

Ten minutes later, Cisco slid over the windowsill to find Poppy crouched once more at her listening post by the door.

With a bad case of the real shivers, not the playacting kind.

15

TO THE SMITH CHILDREN, MEALS AT the Docketts' dining table had from the first seemed as oddly quiet as everything else that went on in the Dockett house, but the silence at breakfast the next morning was more than odd. Only Danny, who was too busy eating, seemed not to notice.

J.D. munched his toast in silence. Cisco and Poppy were busy counting the minutes until nine-thirty, when Ms. Cooperman was expected. The other children slid curious looks at them, and then tried to pretend they were looking out the window or into the kitchen instead. Babba picked at her food and sulked because Cisco and Poppy had told her she would have to give Peachie's locket back when they left. Not even Peachie had much to say, though she dished out scrambled eggs and poured orange juice with her usual cheery little comments.

171

Peachie was in the kitchen when the telephone rang. J.D. went into the living room to answer it. His voice rumbled dimly from beyond the door, but Cisco couldn't make out the words. He wasn't the only one trying. Other times when both J.D. and Peachie were out of a room at the same time there was a low buzz of talk, but not this morning. It was as if they were all waiting for something important—or awful. Even the Three Monkeys had their eyes on their toast and scrambled eggs and their ears cocked. Cisco met Poppy's questioning glance and shrugged. She nodded in the direction of the clock on the dining-room wall and sent him a nervous smile.

Eight twenty-seven.

An hour and three minutes to go.

Poppy's smile wavered as she looked across the table and saw the smug, satisfied smile on Sugar's usually sour face. And not even friendly Tina would meet her eyes. Cisco, if he noticed anything, stubbornly pretended he didn't. Another hour and two minutes and he would be spilling the beans about what must be the weirdest burglary ring in the history of the city of Los Angeles. And he, Cisco Smith, had tiptoed his way right into the cavern where the loot was stored. Right under the nose of the chief thief!

J.D. wore a worried look as he came back into the dining room. He sat down again heavily in his chair at the head of the table.

172

Peachie, coming in from the kitchen with a freshly filled pitcher, stopped so suddenly that orange juice splashed on the floor.

"J.D., honey, what's wrong? Oh, I can just tell it's something awful! What is it?"

J.D. held up both hands as if to calm her down. "Now, now, Peaches, don't get yourself in a swivet. It's not awful for us. Not a bit. But I'm afraid it's unhappy news for Francisco and Poppy and the two little ones. Still, maybe it isn't really as bad as—"

Cisco felt as if somebody had poured ice water down his back. "Was it Ms. Cooperman?" he burst out. "It was, wasn't it?"

Poppy shrank back into her chair as if she didn't want to hear. But she didn't look at all surprised.

J.D. nodded solemnly and reached one big hand out to pat Cisco's. "It was. And I'm afraid she won't be comin' over to fetch you kids this morning after all. She's got some good news and some bad. Seems your momma perked up enough after a good night's rest to get out of the hospital, but—"

"Mom!" Danny bounced up and down excitedly on his chair. "I wanna go see Mom."

"Me too!" Babba cried. Poppy would have bounced up and down herself, but Cisco gave her a sharp nudge. He was waiting for the "but" and the bad news.

"But what?" he demanded.

J.D. hemmed and hawed and gave Cisco's hand another awkward pat. "Ah, hrm, um. I'm sorry, but I don't know any easy way to tell you this, boy. It seems your momma checked herself out of the hospital, and then up and disappeared. Never went back to that campground place. Never said where she was headed for. Just took off. Phhht!"

Poppy went as white as the stripes across her T-shirt. Cisco spoke up in a nervous croak.

"She didn't either! It's not true. She wouldn't do that. She wouldn't go off without us. Not even to go be with Daddy," he insisted angrily.

J.D.'s long face grew gloomier still. "Your Ms. Cooperman says nobody can find him, either. These things happen. I know it's real scary for you kids, but it happens all the time. Folks can only worry on for just so long without money enough to keep a roof over their heads and feed their kiddies. Then the old rubber band snaps."

His pale eyes flicked from Cisco to Poppy and Babba and Danny and then back again. Cisco was so angry that he didn't notice, but Poppy did. It was a crafty look, a puzzling Have-I-scared-you-enough-yet? look.

"*I want Momma!*" Babba shrieked.

Danny started to blubber, and pushed Peachie away when she tried to cuddle him quiet. "Wanna see Mom-mom-*momma*," he sobbed.

174

Peachie swooped around the end of the table to scoop Babba up in a cushiony hug. "You poor, dear, dear little sweeties! Don't you worry. Peachie'll take care of you. Why, I'll bet you it's not even true. I'll bet your momma's just gone looking for a place where you can all be together. An' till she finds one, you'll have good old J.D. an' Peachie to look after you."

The look she gave Cisco and Poppy wasn't half so cheerful. "J.D.'s right, kids. Happens all the time. Fact is, the same thing happened to our Tina and Tim. Last year, just before we moved here. Isn't that right, my dearies?"

The twins nodded. Timmy's chin quivered for a moment, until Tina reached out to clasp his hand.

"Tell you what," Peachie said with a clap of her hands. "We'll call up our friends the Cooleys and one night soon we'll have us a superdeluxe game of Snatch over at their house. That'll give us all something to look forward to."

Cisco thought fast. "C-can we go to our room?" He rubbed at his eyes and tried to look miserable, but inside he felt like dancing a jig because suddenly he understood everything. "We'll come back down and finish our breakfast," he promised quickly when Peachie opened her mouth to protest.

"All right, then," she cooed. "'Course you can. You all just go along and have a good cry and cuddle, and I'll just go see if I can't find us all a special treat in the freezer for lunch."

"Of course it's not true. It's a smelly old lie!" Cisco kept his voice to a whisper as the four children huddled together on Babba's bunk. "Ms. Cooperman wasn't even on the telephone. It was a trick. All the kids knew something was up. They were almost holding their breath. And while they were being real quiet, *I heard Peachie hang up the telephone in the kitchen.*"

Poppy blinked. "Maybe she was just listening in."

"Then why *stop* listening right off?" Cisco asked. "No. I bet she called their own number, and as soon as J.D. answered she hung up. I bet Ms. Cooperman doesn't even know where we are. Poppy's right. J.D. and Peachie are crooks. That first place they took us? With the swimming pool and tennis court? I bet that's the place where they told Ms. Cooperman they lived. And they brought us here all that long, twisty way so *we* wouldn't know where here is."

Babba's eyes grew round. "You mean they stealed us?" she whispered.

" 'Stole,' " Poppy corrected. Cisco nodded.

"And they want to make us all burglars," Poppy breathed. "Last night we were burglars—but only sort of."

"I am *not* a burgular," Babba pouted. "Peachie tricked us. Like you 'splained."

176

Cisco gave her a hug. "That's right. And now they want us to think Mom's off by herself somewhere and doesn't want us with her. Sort of like Hansel and Gretel's mother and father being poor and wanting to get rid of their kids. J.D. and Peachie'd like us to think that so we'll like them better and want to do what they say. But they don't know Mom. And they don't know about Boo. They think there's just the four of us."

"Can we push Peachie in the noven, like the wicked ol' witch?" Danny asked hopefully.

"No. And we've got to pretend we don't know she's a witch," Poppy warned. She made a face. "Pretend she's a nice lady and J.D.'s a nice man."

"I won't." Danny sulked, all the chocolate ice cream forgotten.

"You will too," Cisco said sternly. "Because then they won't guess we're going to escape."

"Es-escape?" Poppy's voice faltered. "Where to? We don't know where we are."

Babba looked surprised. "Yes we do."

Cisco frowned. "No we don't."

"*I* do," Babba said.

16

AFTER BREAKFAST ON SATURDAY MORN-
ing, Boo went out to sit on the curb in front of
the Maldonados' house and think. There had to
be *something* she could do. All day Friday she had
sat around watching TV and fidgeting. If
only . . . If only she could remember where she
had seen the plum-red van with the elephant dent
on it. It had to be the fake Dickerys'. There
couldn't be *two* such vans.

Maybe Auntie had remembered where she saw
it—unless she had been making that up to make
Boo feel better. But Auntie had been back at the
campground since Thursday evening. She had
wanted to spend that night at the open-24-hours
laundromat down on Figueroa Street, but the two
policemen who came to ask for photographs of
the missing Smith children had offered her a ride
downtown. The policemen called her 'Granny,'
which made her scowl, and bullied her in a
friendly, joking way into going even though she

178

didn't want to. She left all but two of her plastic bags in Elvira and went off in a sulk in the squad car.

When the policemen first phoned to ask about the photographs, Mr. Maldonado and his son Rudy had gone out to Elvira with Boo and shifted the mattresses so she could get at the apple carton that held the Smiths' scrapbook and Cisco and Poppy's school photos. Except for baby pictures taken at a department store, there were no photos of Babba and Danny. The Smiths didn't have a camera. Mrs. Maldonado went through her own photos, though, and found several of all of the children together. The policemen took two of those and the school photos, and asked a lot of questions about how old and how tall the children were and what clothes they were wearing on Wednesday. But when Boo and Mr. and Mrs. Maldonado asked what the police were doing to find them, all they would say was, "We're doing everything that can be done." Which either meant they didn't have a clue or, as Mr. Maldonado said afterward, they figured what they knew was nobody's business but their own and Mr. Smith's. And Boo's father wasn't due in from Pittsburgh until Sunday morning.

Worst of all—much worse than being smiled at absentmindedly or talked about as if she wasn't in the room—they didn't believe Boo's clue. First they asked how she knew about the Dickerys' van.

Then they said snooping around at the house in Hancock Park was interference with a police investigation. And they ended up smiling vaguely and saying it was probably wishful thinking and she'd never really seen such a van. It was after Auntie said that she had seen it somewhere too that they started asking her a lot of questions and found out that she wasn't really anybody's aunt at all, but the famous loudmouthed Highland Park Wagon Lady. After that Boo could tell that they thought the old lady wouldn't know a van from a ham sandwich.

The screen door banged as Mrs. Maldonado came out onto the front porch. "Eh, Boo!" she called. "You sit out there much longer, you'll put down roots. Come have a glass of lemonade."

"Okay." Boo sighed and dawdled back across the lawn. The sun was growing too hot for curb sitting anyway.

Mrs. Maldonado gave Boo's blouse and shorts a critical look as she poured lemonade into a tall, ice-filled glass. "Tch! It looks as if those must have been rolled up and packed into a Band-Aid box. You'd better pick out what you want to wear tomorrow morning so I can iron it today. You will not want to look like something out of a laundry basket when you go to meet the airplane, I think."

"No." Boo's heart gave a leap. "But I thought Daddy was coming from the airport on the bus."

Mrs. Maldonado smiled as she handed Boo the

glass. "Ah, I thought that would erase even such a black frown. No, first the airport bus and then changing buses downtown, and walking up from Figueroa Street? It would take hours. But our Rudy says he does not mind at all driving on the freeways, and that he will go to meet the airplane. The sooner your father is here, the better."

Lemonade sloshed out of Boo's glass as she set it down on the porch railing and flung her arms around Mrs. Maldonado's stout waist. "Oh, *thank you!* I can't wait," she cried, but in the next moment Mrs. Maldonado's clean-laundry-and-fresh-baked-bread-smelling hug proved too much for her and she was sobbing into her comfortable bosom the first tears she had dared to shed. It was *hard* being twelve and the oldest.

"There now, there now! That's what comes of moping half the morning away," Mrs. Maldonado scolded kindly. "If you don't want to watch TV, why not read something? There's stories in some of the magazines in on the coffee table."

Boo had already looked, but the only thing besides Rudy's kids' Donald Duck comics and Mrs. Maldonado's *Family Circle*s was the new July *National Geographic,* and she had read that last week right after Mr. Maldonado finished it.

"No?" Mrs. Maldonado gave Boo a shrewd look. "Well, I wouldn't be surprised if they didn't have something you'd like in the paperback rack down at the Monty Market. We will make a bargain. You can save me a trip down the hill for the three or four sweet red peppers and two cans of the big, black olives I need for our rice and chicken for tonight, and I will give you money for a book."

Boo dried her eyes with the back of her hand. "Lucky's cheaper," she said with a sniffle.

"Ay, but it is so much farther!"

"That's okay," Boo said. "What time's lunch?"

"In about two hours," Mrs. Maldonado answered. "But if you are back in time you can go with Rudy and his family to Griffith Park. They are taking a picnic and then will go to the Zoo."

"I don't feel zooish," Boo said. What she really didn't feel like was spending the day with Rudy and Linda's little kids. When she was around them all she could think of was Danny and Babba.

Coming back down the slope of the Lucky Food Center's parking lot to Figueroa Street, Boo zigzagged between the cars, drawn by the Winchell's Donut House at the lower corner. She had already read all of the kids' books in the Lucky paperback racks that looked halfway interesting, so had settled for the new *Archie* comic instead. And since it cost only half as much as a book, there was enough change left for a puffy glazed doughnut and a Coke. But at the last minute, stepping back against a van as a bright yellow pickup truck looking for a parking space turned across her path, she hesitated. After all, doughnuts and Cokes were for eating, not reading.

Which meant the change was really all still Mrs. Maldonado's.

In the end neither Boo's conscience nor the tempting aroma that wafted out through the donut shop's door won. Instead, she saw—as she might not have if she had made a beeline for Hobart Street—a familiar figure, shopping bag in either hand, stumping its way up the sidewalk on the opposite side of Figueroa Street.

"Auntie!" Boo shrieked. Darting down to the curb, she waved eagerly. *"Auntie!"*

Old Mrs. Moss wheeled around in a circle, looking to see where the call had come from. She waved back when she caught sight of Boo.

Boo hurried to the corner, and as soon as the traffic lights changed, she clutched the bag with the peppers and olives to her chest and made a dash for the other side.

"What are you doing back here?" she asked breathlessly.

Auntie scowled at her dusty sandals. "Blamed if I know, now. I got a ride far as Avenue Twenty-six, but my feet feel like I been walking for hours." She scratched her nose. "It was that van got to niggling at me. We mighta seen it downtown somewheres, so yesterday I talked to a couple of friends who live on the street. They said they'd put out the word that everybody should keep an eye peeled for it. But I still didn't get a wink of sleep all last night for thinking about it. I just got it in my head it was up around here I saw it, maybe a week, two weeks ago. Anyhow, I didn't like not knowing about the kids and your mom. So here I am, foot blisters and all. You had any news from the cops yet?"

"Nope." Boo matched her stride to the old woman's slower pace as they came to the shady stretch along the edge of Sycamore Grove Park. "I wish they'd find the kids quick. *Today.* Before Daddy gets here and has to tell Mom what happened. But I don't think they even listened about the van."

"Never you mind," Auntie said firmly. She gave Boo's shoulder an awkward pat. "If it lives around here, all I got to do is stick close to Figueroa, say from the park here up to Avenue Fifty-four, and I'll spot it sooner or later. Then we'll—*OW!* That's my *foot,* you . . . " She broke off abruptly as Boo tugged frantically at the sleeve of her sweater. "What is it? Boo? What's the matter?"

Boo nodded violently up the street, speechless for a moment in alarm and surprise. Then, "The van," she whispered hoarsely. "That's it! That's *it.* It must have been in the parking lot at Lucky."

The van, a plum-red Chevrolet with windows along its sides and a large dent that looked amazingly like an elephant on its side door, was not moving fast, but already it was fifty or sixty yards off. It followed the curve of traffic as Figueroa Street climbed away from the park.

"Then what the blazes are you standing here gawping for, peanut brain?" the old woman snapped. She gave Boo a hard shove. "The license number, for Pete's sake. Run! Get the blasted license number!"

Boo ran faster than she ever had, faster than she thought she could. She flew. Still the van pulled steadily away, with a small blue car crowding so close behind that it hid the license plate. A moment later, dodging a woman pushing a baby stroller, she saw the plum-colored van's roof again, stopped in the line of traffic backed up by a red light at Avenue 52. But the light changed too soon, and the plum-red roof moved on. Boo streaked past the little Plaza shops and on so fast that the car-dealer–car-wash–Pioneer-Chicken–7-Eleven–Avenue-52-Buddhist-Temple–Southwest-Motors were only a blur. But beyond Southwest Motors she came to a dead stop.

The van had vanished.

"Hey there, Belinda! Belinda Smith!" Mr. Monahan appeared in the car showroom doorway. "Bless me," he exclaimed, "you were really burning up the sidewalk there. Where's the fire? And what's all this in the paper this morning about Cisco and the little ones?"

"A plum van. Plum colored," Boo panted. "Did you see it? Just now. It's got this big ding on its side like an elephant and it's the one the kids got stolen away in. I know it is!"

Mr. Monahan's friendly-salesman look vanished. His eyes narrowed. "Just now? No. But we've had a plum-red van with a dent like that in here for service. I'm sure of it. Come on out back and we'll ask Pat."

"No. I've got to get the license number," Boo said wildly. "I've got to find out where it goes." Wheeling, she raced back toward the stop light. Downhill on Avenue 52 toward the freeway entrance there was no car or van in sight. In the opposite direction Boo saw two cars moving uphill and a row of others parked along the curb, but no plum-colored van.

Mr. Monahan came puffing up to the corner, waving a piece of paper. "No luck? Don't you . . . worry," he panted. "I was right. Your dad's buddies . . . back in the service department . . . remember the van. Plum-red 1985 Dodge Ram van. It came in for a body-work estimate on that dent." He drew a deep breath. "We've got the license number right here on the estimate form: 3HKM600. Pat Markle's calling the cops."

An old man waiting on the corner for the light to change turned to peer at them curiously.

"You looking for a van like that? Sounds like one that passed me a coupla minutes ago. Going down that way." He pointed down Avenue 52 toward the freeway entrance.

Boo's heart sank.

17

BOO WAS NOT DOWNHEARTED FOR long. After all, if the plum-colored van shopped for groceries at Lucky and might be getting its dent fixed at Southwest Motors, it stood to reason that it lived nearby. Or at least not very far off.

"What's on the other side of the bridge?" Boo asked quickly as she caught sight of Auntie panting up Figueroa Street. She hoped Mr. Monahan hadn't seen. He didn't like "tramps" and once had called the police to come and move old Mrs. Moss on when she decided to park her wagon and have a picnic lunch on the sidewalk in front of his main showroom window.

Boo had never given a thought to there being anything at all beyond the bridge over the freeway and the dry riverbed of the Arroyo Seco. She had never walked down that way—going anywhere near the freeway was against Smith rules—and had supposed that the street just stopped right there at the foot of the steep slope of the high hummock of hill beyond. But that was silly. If the road wasn't going somewhere, there wouldn't be a bridge.

"Over there? That's Debs Park." Mr. Monahan fixed a sharp eye on Auntie Moss while she waited on the corner across the way for the traffic light to change. "Street takes a sharp right turn and runs on down the Arroyo," he said shortly. "Once you get around the corner it's Griffin Avenue, not Avenue Fifty-two. Takes you down into Montecito Heights. Huh! Now what's that old battle-ax got her beady eye on me for?"

Boo had forgotten Auntie again, and Mrs. Maldonado's peppers and olives—and even the unpleasant tightness at the bottom of her stomach that had been there from the moment she heard Ms. Cooperman say about the children, "They've vanished too." For as long as it took to run a bit more than half a mile, she had been *doing* something. But now what could she do? With both the freeway and Griffin Avenue at the bottom of Avenue 52, the kidnappers' van could get just about anywhere. And be *from* just about anywhere. Crooks did things for crooked reasons. Maybe they shopped at Lucky and decided to get the van repaired at Southwest Motors because those places *weren't* near home.

"Auntie Moss? It's me she wants." Boo was determined not to cry, but she couldn't help one small sniffle. "She's got my groceries. Mrs.

Maldonado's, I mean. I'm s'posed to go back for lunch." She made a sign to Auntie not to cross when the light changed.

"I'd better get back myself," Mr. Monahan said. "Find out from Pat what the police had to say. I'll give the Maldonados a ring if I hear anything." He pulled out the crisp, blue handkerchief that peeped from the breast pocket of his sports jacket.

"Here, you take this for those sniffles, Belinda honey. But—" His voice sharpened. "Don't let that old she-fraud get hold of it or I'll never get it back."

"What're you so down in the mouth for?" Auntie had said when she heard about the van. "You don't s'pose old Lady Luck's gonna hand over your brats on a silver platter, do you? Look, you go grab that good lunch, and I'll hike down over the bridge and park myself somewheres near the road and have me a peanut-butter-and-crackers picnic. If Mrs. M. says it's okay, come on down and we'll have us a prowl around."

To Boo's surprise, Mrs. Maldonado did say it was OK.

"To tell the truth," she said as she rinsed the last of the dishes from lunch and placed it in the rack for Boo to dry, "I do not think it likely that you will find that van, but it is good for the heart

189

to be doing something. And you will be safe with Florence. Auntie, that is. She has grown wise in the ways of stepping aside from trouble."

"What did she used to be like?" Boo asked, suddenly curious. "When she lived next door." She had never even wondered before.

Mrs. Maldonado thought for a moment and then, raising her eyebrows in surprise, said. "Much like the day before yesterday. I thought it was only that for once she looked almost clean and tidy, but no. She did not talk so loudly, or abuse the policemen. Perhaps, perhaps a small blessing comes from your great difficulties. Perhaps her concern for your mother and the children has drawn her so far out of her unhappiness that she begins to awaken to her old self. I hope so. I liked the old Florence. Her tongue was sharp, but her heart soft."

"Come." Mrs. Maldonado dried her hands and took the dishtowel from Boo. "Cut a piece of the cake to take to her. The waxed paper to wrap it in is there, on the counter. I will finish the drying."

At the stop sign before the bridge over the freeway, Boo looked both ways twice at the crosswalk. Then she made a dash across the freeway approach road. There was no car in sight, but cars could spring out of nowhere. On the bridge itself she hurried along at the left edge of the sidewalk, close to the curb so that she couldn't see down over the parapet to the rushing cars below. High places left Boo's knees feeling wobbly.

But in the middle of the bridge Boo forgot the cars, her knees, and Auntie munching on crackers somewhere around the corner on Griffin Avenue. Cisco's clues. The pins! She had completely forgotten the pins. After finding the first two, finding any more had seemed hopeless because the plum-colored van might have gone anywhere. But if the van had come here . . .

If. If it had come here by freeway, it could have left the freeway by this very exit.

If that was so, and if Cisco had known that they were on a freeway turn-off—and if he had any pins left by then—he *must* have dropped a clue. Cisco just would. He would be spinning plans for escape, pretending he was some TV hero captured by dastardly villains. Cisco's head was always as full of plots and plans as Boo's was of daydreams. Boo was sorry now that she had made fun of his plots. So what if a lot of them were silly? If silliness worked . . .

A car coming up from the freeway exit paused at the stop sign ahead and then turned left. As soon as it had passed, Boo crossed the road to the sign and, holding onto it, climbed over the metal guard rail into the shrubbery. It was a tight squeeze, and as she moved down around the long

191

curve, eyes on the road, the bushes snagged her T-shirt and scratched at her bare legs. Cars rushed past, some of them so fast that even with the guard rail for protection, Boo shrank back in alarm. One slowed down and a man leaned over to yell out the window, "You better get out of there before a cop sees you, kid."

Boo hurried down through the shrubbery as far as she dared go, eyes still on the roadway. What if she spied a pin out there? She wouldn't dare climb over the guard rail to try to pick it up. Not without a policeman to stop the cars. And what policeman was going to believe her about the clue, and not just say, "Now don't you worry, kid. Everything's being done that can be done"?

But there were no pins. No pin. On the way back up the slope Boo walked head down, watching the ground as she scuffed her feet through the dusty earth. A pin *could* bounce right under the guard rail. Or even over it.

It was a gloomy Boo who swung around the stop sign and made her way around the curve onto Griffin Avenue. There were no houses, only hillside and the roadside strip of park. She found Auntie sitting in a patch of grass with a piece of newspaper spread out for a tablecloth, using a stick to spread peanut butter on her last cracker.

"Where the—where the Sam Hill've you been?" Auntie called. She fished in her skirt pocket and held out her hand. "Come lookit what I found back there by that stop sign."

Boo snatched at the pins. There were two of them, fastened together as before: one of the cartoon character Roadrunner and the other a little ram's-head emblem of the Los Angeles Rams football team.

"They're Cisco's. They are! I don't know what Roadrunner's s'posed to mean, but Mr. Monahan called that van a Ram van." Boo closed her fist around them and hugged them to her chest. "Oh, gosh. What should we do now?"

Auntie thought for a moment. "Tell you what," she said. "You take 'em and zip back to that fat guy at the car place, that Pete Monahan. Tell him you found 'em, and get him to tell the cops. If I tried, they'd hoot me right off the phone. They'll listen to Monahan."

Boo fumbled to fasten the pins to the lining of the pocket in her shorts for safety. "What are you going to do?"

Auntie scratched her ear. "I've got this hunch," she said. "Anybody coming from over by that Chiltern Place place wouldn't come off the freeway at Avenue Fifty-two and turn down a road that goes right back the way they'd come—not unless they're being foxy, maybe keeping clear of some freeway exit that's real close to wherever it is they're heading for. And the exit down at Avenue Forty-three's the only one near here. Over

193

on this side of the freeway, Forty-three toots right up into Montecito Heights, so I figure I'll head down that way. I'll keep my eyes peeled for more of those little doodads. Maybe ask at the Griffin Avenue Market if anybody's seen that van."

The old woman pushed herself awkwardly to her feet. "Well, what are you waiting for?" She scowled. "Hop to it!"

18

THE TERRIBLE SATURDAY-MORNING breakfast at the Dockett house had been followed by Seek and a new game, Gotcha! In Gotcha! the players tried to sneak past a blindfolded "It" without being detected—another burglary lesson pretending to be a game.

"You were real good all morning, but don't forget," Cisco warned in a whisper as the four Smith children got ready to follow the others downstairs after washing their hands for lunch. "Nobody says *any*thing about burglars. Not. A. Thing. Okay, Babba?"

Babba looked almost miserable, which for Babba was something new. Keeping her mouth shut was hard work. "What'll happen if I forget an' tell?" she asked.

"Something awful." Cisco looked so gloomy that even Danny gulped.

"W-Will they lock us in the cellar?"

Cisco considered. "No. I guess what they'd do

is load us up in their old van and take us where we'd never *ever* be able to find out where we were. Or find our way home." He said it because it was the scariest thing he could think of for keeping two small mouths shut, but as the words came out his own heart went *b-bump!* It was just what J.D. and Peachie might do.

"I do know where we are!" Babba stopped on the top step and stamped her foot. "I *tol'* you," she squeaked. "We're 'cross from the house that sticks up on the hill."

"Maybe—" Poppy began.

Cisco sighed. "Don't be silly. She just made that up. Babba's too little to see anything out the attic windows. She isn't even as tall as the window sills. Besides, there are shutters on the bottom part of the windows up there, just like everywhere else. Now, come on, or Peachie'll be mad."

To everyone's surprise except perhaps Peachie's, J.D. was home from "work" and sitting in his high-backed chair at the head of the dining-room table.

"Thought I'd take the afternoon off," he announced as he flapped his napkin open and tucked one corner into his belt. "Peachie says y'all have got so good at Sneak and Seek and Snatch that I figured I ought to come have a look-see. Maybe like Peachie says it's time to have us a game of Super Snatch, and this time I'll come along.

Just the ticket to cheer us all up after the unhappy news the Smith kids here had this morning about their mom." He picked up a fork and attacked his macaroni and cheese with gusto.

Poppy paled and passed the serving bowl without taking any.

"Something wrong, sweetie?" Peachie gave her a sharp look.

J.D. had his eye on Cisco. "How's that sound to you, Francisco?"

"Me?" Cisco's voice squeaked. "Great. It sounds great."

It sounded awful. Terrible. If they went burgling again now that they knew it was burgling, then even if they escaped or were rescued, they wouldn't get to go to Grandma's in Pittsburgh. Not ever. They would be stuck, either with J.D. and Peachie, or in jail. Jail, or wherever it was that they put burglar kids.

"Well then, that's settled." J.D. smiled his wolfish smile and then licked his lips. "This's good macaroni, Peaches. Lots of cheese, just the way I like it. Better serve up some more for Francisco and Poppy here, though. There's not enough on their plates to feed a canary bird."

The plateful that Peachie dished out was almost more than Cisco, frightened as he was, could bear to look at. But though the "bad news" at breakfast made it all right to look gloomy, it wasn't safe to let J.D. suspect he thought there was anything

197

wrong in going out on a "game of Snatch." He picked up his fork to stab at the macaroni, and ate until J.D.'s watchful eye wandered off across the table. He started up again when it wandered back. But before long Cisco discovered to his surprise that he had only a forkful or two left and had almost finished a glassful of lemonade. He was getting as piggy as Danny. Still, it was very, very good macaroni, made with real cheese, not the orangey-powder imitation kind, and the lemonade had real lemons and real sugar in it. Feeling guilty, Cisco wished that Peachie wasn't such a good cook. If only the macaroni were gluey and the lemonade fake and there were no ice cream to come, it would be a lot easier to concentrate on thinking up a good escape plan.

Poppy had eaten a little bit, but mostly she just cut the macaroni into little pieces with her fork and pushed them around on her plate. But not even Poppy could resist strawberry ice cream for dessert. By the time she got down to the last spoonful, her sad look had turned almost dreamy, as if she were wondering whether there would be ice cream for lunch in Pittsburgh.

There sure wouldn't be any in jail.

Up in the attic playroom, J.D. sat himself on a folding chair, with his big, hairy hands on his wide-spread knees, as if to say, "Think you're good, do you? All right, show me!" Peachie came tripping up the stairs last in line, with her tablet and pencils and timekeeper's clock.

"Now, don't you all let me down." She patted the head of each of the young Smiths as she passed. "You show J.D. you're every little bit as good at Sneak as I bragged to him."

The hopeful look Poppy had worn coming up the stairs vanished as she looked around the big, open attic room. Cisco, following her glance, saw it move from one high-silled, shuttered window to the next, and come back to rest on Babba. The only thing to be seen out the unshuttered upper half of each window was the sky.

"I told you," he hissed.

All eleven children fell silent as Peachie settled herself and held up her hand.

Chuckie went first. Cisco tried hard to look interested, but inside he felt as dithery and alarmed as Poppy looked. Should he try to do really well at the climbing and balancing and crawling and wriggling so that J.D. would think he truly wanted to go out Snatching and wouldn't watch him so sharply? Or should he flub it up so that J.D. figured he might flub up the burgling too?

The *Go* signal for Cisco's turn on the Sneak obstacle course came while he was still dithering. Startled, he jumped for the climbing rope and went swarming up from knot to knot as fast as he could go. By the time he reached the tangle of the jungle gym, he decided that just a little bit of noise would be safer than a real flub.

It was then, balanced on top of the jungle gym, that he glanced out the upper part of the window straight ahead and hesitated for a fraction of a second in surprise. In that moment one foot slipped, and his knee caught against the bar with a painful smack. Catching at the next bar, he scrambled up and across and hopped down to the floor and into the plastic pipe in a daze. He did not hear the click of Peachie's timer as he came wriggling out at the far end, or see J.D. lean over to read the dial and then give him an unpleasant hard-eyed look.

One anxious glance at Cisco told Poppy that something was up. As Tina started her turn at the obstacle course, Poppy began to edge out of line. Turning so that his hand was out of J.D.'s sight, Cisco made a frantic sign for her to stay where she was. His next sign meant "I'll tell you later." Poppy looked puzzled but stayed where she was.

Turning away, Cisco pretended to watch Tina. He tried hard to look calm, but inside he was shivering with excitement. He hardly felt the pain in his knee. Then, out of the corner of his eye, he saw J.D. looming at his elbow. J.D.'s heavy hand clapped down on his shoulder.

"Not a bad try, Francisco. Not bad," he said softly. "Only it's not so easy to fool old J.D."

Startled, Cisco stuttered, "W-w-what?" J.D.'s smile was broad, but his gray eyes were narrow and chilly. His smile was so wide that his eyeteeth showed, long and pointy, but his eyes were scary. They looked at Cisco almost as if they could read the thoughts inside his head.

"It won't work, young man." J.D. shook his head. "It was a convincing fall, and that's a real good limp, but it won't get you out of this next Snatch. I'm onto you." He gave Cisco's shoulder a sharp shake. "Even if that fall was real and we had to leave you behind, Poppy and the two kiddies would go."

"I don't know what you mean," Cisco mumbled. He tried to pull away.

"Oh, you know what I mean, all right." J.D.'s grasp was as hard as a vise. "Didn't think about dust, did you?" he whispered. "Peachie's been after me all week to get that van washed. So I go out to the garage this morning and take a gander at it, and you coulda knocked me over with a feather. Hand and footprints all over the roof! Now, how do you suppose they got there? Or up on the rafters?"

Freeing Cisco's shoulder, he gave him a pat on the back.

"Don't you worry about it, now. You'll do all right. Peachie and me, we like a sharp, snoopy kid. Just what we need in our business."

As he moved away, Cisco shivered. Now they

had to get away. Fast. At least—at last!—he did know where they were.

For, looking out through the upper part of the window, he had seen in the distance a white, Spanish-style building with a stumpy tower— Babba's "big, white house that sticks up on the hill."

It was the Southwest Museum on the hillside above Figueroa Street.

19

CISCO TOLD POPPY THE GOOD NEWS AS they climbed the stairway from the downstairs hall.

Poppy was close on his heels as he reached the top. *"Honest?"* She stopped and stared. "That's what Babba saw? That big building up on the hill? The museum with all the Indian stuff in it? Then—" Her voice wobbled. "Then, we're almost home. We can go to Mrs. Maldonado's house. I bet that's where Boo is."

Cisco flapped his hands at her in warning. "Not so loud," he hissed. "J.D. and Peachie don't know we lived on Hobart Street. If they find out, they'll—they'll pack us all up and take us away, just like I bet they took the other kids clear away from where they snatched them."

"But we'll get out before that," Poppy said eagerly. She caught at Cisco's T-shirt. "Can we try right now? I can go find Babba and Danny—"

"No!" Cisco spoke sharply. "I mean, not yet."

Ducking into the bedroom George shared with the Three Monkeys, he headed for the chest of drawers. Poppy followed and watched as he pulled out the bottom drawer and felt around on the floor inside until he came up with a shiny new quarter. With the Sneak game finished, J.D. and Peachie had started the children on a new sort of game of Seek: a search for good hiding places. More burglary lessons, Cisco knew now. He had already found seventy-five cents. Poppy was too excited even to think about looking.

"When, then? While Peachie's getting dinner?" Poppy asked eagerly.

Cisco turned back toward the door. "Look, I don't know," he whispered impatiently. Then with a look of alarm he jumped back as his hand touched the doorknob. The knob was already moving.

It was George who stuck his head in. He looked gloomier than ever. "Oh. Where'd you look? Under the chest of drawers?" He went to feel under the pillows on the bunks, but finding nothing, turned to say shyly, "You found out, didn't you? About the burgling? Peachie says we don't need to keep our mouths shut anymore."

Poppy was alarmed. "How'd she find out we know?"

Cisco made a face. "That was the bad news. J.D. found out I saw all the burgled stuff. He found my footprints on top of the van where I climbed over, and figured they had to be mine.

How dumb can you get? I never thought about the dust."

"You're not gonna make a stink, are you?" George asked. "If you do like they say, lots of the time they're not so bad. Honest."

Cisco and Poppy were silent.

"Okay," George said awkwardly. "I guess I'll go check some more hiding places."

Cisco and Poppy followed him into the hall. As he vanished around a corner, Poppy said, "I *will* go find Babba and Danny. You think up a plan for how we're going to get out."

"I can't think up a plan," Cisco hissed, almost as if he were angry at Poppy instead of J.D. and Peachie. "The wall's too high to climb. And the ladder's too heavy and we don't know where the 'lectronic gate doohickey is. Nobody can open the gate except J.D. or Peachie, and they're not gonna open it until tonight when we're all shut up in the van, ready to go out and do some more burgly-snatch."

Danny's funny word didn't make Poppy smile. Instead, she burst into tears. "I *won't* go be a burglar. I won't!" She stamped her foot Babba-fashion.

"Shut up!" Cisco growled unhappily. He turned fearfully to look back along the hallway. None of the other players in the Seek game were in sight, but J.D. or Peachie might pop up anywhere without warning.

Opening the door to Sugar's bedroom, he

205

pulled Poppy in and shut the door after them. "J.D.'ll get mad if he hears, and he's scary enough when he's being nice." Cisco shivered.

Poppy sniffled. "Well, you go be a burglar, then. *I* won't."

"Me neither. But we need a plan. I *had* a plan." Cisco kicked at Sugar's wastebasket. "But it won't work. You know the pine trees over on the other side of the driveway? If we climbed all the way up to the top like Babba and Danny used to do at home, the branches grow so close together that nobody could get us down if we didn't want to come. We could yell to the neighbors to go call the police. But you're scared to climb trees."

Poppy swallowed. "I . . . I could try."

Cisco shook his head. "You'd just freeze partway up, like old Motorboat did that time Mr. Maldonado had to call the fire department to get him down off the telephone pole. Then I had this other plan, that we'd get out on the front-porch roof from in here and jump across into the tree that grows right by the fence."

He moved to the window and opened the shutters to point to the big magnolia tree. "The big branch on the other side hangs out over the sidewalk. But it's too far for Danny to jump. Or Babba." He kicked at Sugar's wastebasket again, and it turned over, spilling lipsticky tissues onto the carpet. Cisco was glad to have an excuse to get down on the floor and not have to look Poppy in the eye. It was bad enough that he had been almost as dazzled as greedy Babba by the Docketts' goodies—all the TV and video and games and food—but now that he knew what had to be done, he couldn't think up a way to do it. All he could think was how easy it would be to escape if he were alone. Escapers in the movies or on TV never had little brothers or sisters to worry about.

"Don't feel bad," Poppy said loyally. "You thought up about dropping the pins. That was a good idea."

"It was a dumb idea." And all but eleven of his precious pins were gone.

"*I* think it was a good one." Poppy screwed her eyes up and thought fiercely. "I know!" she said suddenly.

Cisco put the wastebasket back beside Sugar's dressing table. "You know what?"

"What we can do. We can write a note that says Peachie and J.D. made us do it, and tell where we are. And leave it where the people who get burgled can find it."

Cisco looked at his kid sister in surprise. Maybe it wasn't an exciting idea, but it was good. And safe. Most important of all, it could really work.

"That's good. Yes! And we can tell them J.D. and Peachie's real last name, and I know the license numbers on the vans. And we can tell they stole the other kids too. And how the garage is full of loot, and—" All of a sudden he stopped. "Where are we going to get a piece of paper and a pencil?"

Paper and a pencil. In the Dockett house there seemed to be not only no books and no news-papers, but no tablets, no pens or pencils. It hadn't occurred to Cisco before, but perhaps, if the children never went to school, they couldn't read or write.

"Here." Poppy knelt and tugged at the bottom drawer of Sugar's chest of drawers. Reaching underneath the neatly folded winter skirts and sweaters she pulled out two tacks and tugged free a large sheet of glossy pink paper. "I don't know what it's for, but Peachie has it in her drawers, too," Poppy said. She tore off a wide strip, folded it into a square small enough to fit into her pocket, and stuffed the rest back under the sweaters.

"She won't be looking under there for a long time," Poppy said happily.

That was when Sugar banged the door open.

"Sneaks! How much did you find?" She glared. "Anything you find in my room, I get."

"All the rooms are in the game," Cisco said defiantly. "That's the rules."

"In my room I make the rules." Sugar's eyes narrowed. Crossing the room, she pushed Poppy away from the open drawer and pulled it all the way out so that she could feel around the empty space below. Pocketing the quarter that she found there, she jammed the drawer back in and went to pull out the middle drawer of her dressing table and reach into the space behind. Her hand came out with another quarter. "Short drawer," she explained. "Lots of drawers have a space behind, not just underneath the bottom one. And lots of people hide things behind the books on bookshelves, only we don't have any. *I've* already found two dollars and seventy-five cents, and I bet you the bell rings any minute and I've won." She flounced out of the room.

"The pencil Peachie uses to keep score," Cisco whispered. "Maybe she left it up in the playroom. Come on. We can write the letter when we're s'posed to be getting cleaned up for dinner."

It was a very good letter even though it was a bit messy toward the end, when the pencil was too worn down. Cisco used two of his last eleven pins to fasten the paper at the bottom of Poppy's pocket so it couldn't fall out, no matter what. They agreed that the best place to leave it would be inside a burgled jewelry box, if there was one, and if not, in the burgled silverware drawer.

At dinner, once all of the children heard that the four Smiths knew they had been fooled into taking part in a real burglary, everything changed. Except Sugar. Sugar was bossier and more sour than ever, but the others dropped their almost fearful shyness. Tina even asked Peachie whether she could change her place and sit next to Poppy. As soon as the children were

209

excused from the table, the Three Monkeys took Babba and Danny off to show them the rats' nest in the narrow space between the back of the garage and the tall fence. George proposed that they ask to rearrange the bedroom assignments: George and Cisco and Tim together, Tina and Poppy and Babba in their own bedroom, and Danny in with the Three Monkeys.

"No," Poppy said firmly while Cisco was trying to think of a friendlier way to say the same thing.

Babba and Danny loved the new attention from the others, but remembered to keep a mistrustful distance from J.D. and Peachie. Cisco and Poppy were puzzled by the change until Tina, holding hands with Poppy on the way upstairs at seven-thirty—the early "first" bedtime on Snatch nights—whispered in a happy rush of words, "Peachie says because we all tricked you into going out to play Snatch, you can't tell on us now, because you'd go to jail too. J.D. says the nasty old police put boys and girls in different jails and I'd never get to see Tim again, and they just give you brown bread and bean soup to eat and the beds don't have any mattresses, just bedbugs."

"That's not true!" Cisco scoffed, but then he added uneasily, "At least I bet it isn't." One of the boys in Boo's class had been sent away to Juvenile Hall, but when he got out, his family moved, so Boo never got to hear about the food and beds.

The words "you can't tell now" and "bedbugs" gave Poppy an uncomfortable twinge. Slipping her hand in her pocket, she fingered the note addressed PLEASE GIVE THIS TO THE POLEECE and crossed her fingers. What if it didn't get found before the next burglary? What if the people who lived in tonight's burgled house were off in San Francisco or—or down in Mexico, and it didn't get found for *weeks*?

At fifteen minutes to midnight the last sock was pulled over the last tennis shoe, the last dark sweatshirt hood was tied under the last chin, the last caramel had been handed out, and Peachie held her hand up for silence.

"All right, line up, kids! J.D.'s got the van out by now. And remember: double quiet. We haven't ever waked the neighbors up, so let's not start now." She gave Cisco a sharp look, and then, turning out the hall light, opened the side door and waved the children on out.

The plum-red van, a dark shadow under the car porch's trellis, stood waiting with its doors open and the engine purring. Danny clambered in after Chuckie, but Babba hung back and clung to Poppy, who was clutching Cisco's hand.

"Get a move on!" Peachie hissed. She gave Cisco a sharp poke in the small of his back. "We're wasting time."

Cisco fought back tears. If Poppy wasn't crying,

211

he certainly wasn't going to. He helped Babba up into the van, and then gave Poppy a hand. Danny sat in the front row with the Three Monkeys, but Cisco steered Babba and Poppy toward the seat at the back—the farther away from J.D. and Peachie the better. As he passed the third row of seats, George's hand grasped his wrist and gave a friendly squeeze. At the hum of the opening gate, someone gave a very small sigh in the darkness.

The big van nosed quietly out through the gate, turning left.

And then, suddenly, lights sprang on all around.

There were spotlights ahead. And floodlights. And headlights everywhere. And flashing lights on the tops of police cars. And lights in every house along the street as neighbors switched them on and dashed to their windows to see what was happening.

Police cars were parked in the driveways of the neighbors on both sides of the Docketts' house. Three more police cars blocked the street, and in two others drawn up behind the van, Cisco and Poppy—their noses flattened against the rear window—could make out Boo and Auntie and Ms. Cooperman at the open back-seat windows of one, and Mr. Monahan and Mr. and Mrs. Maldonado in the other.

*   *   *

In the van, J.D. and Peachie sat speechless. Of the children, only Danny found his voice.

"So *there*, Vulpo!" he yelled, and he punched J.D. hard on the shoulder.

20

EVERYONE WENT TO THE AIRPORT ON
Sunday morning: Boo and Cisco and Poppy and
Babba and Danny in Ms. Cooperman's car, Mr.
and Mrs. Maldonado and Rudy's family in Mr.
Maldonado's car, and Auntie Moss on the wide,
comfortable backseat of a long, gray Chrysler driven by an only slightly grumpy Mr. Monahan.
Once the cars were parked, they all trooped
through the terminal and up to the gate through
which the passengers from Mr. Smith's plane
were to come. When he appeared, everyone
cheered, with even the people waiting for other
passengers joining in. Some clapped and cheered
because they had seen reports on the television
news about the rescue of the kidnapped children
and the arrest of the ringleaders of the busiest
burglary ring in the city. Others cheered just because it felt good to see so many people looking
so happy.

The Maldonados rode back home together—

Rudy and Linda and their children were leaving after lunch for San Diego in their camper, and Mrs. Maldonado had to change the sheets on their beds for the Smiths, who would be coming to stay for the two or three nights before they set off for Pittsburgh in Elvira. Ms. Cooperman, happy that for once one of her cases had an ending as happy as it was tidy, offered Auntie a ride downtown to the campground, and wasn't even angry with her about pretending to be the children's aunt. Only Auntie Moss seemed sad that the adventure was over.

Mr. Smith rode with the children in Mr. Monahan's car as it flew across the city by freeway, headed for the County-USC Hospital. In the back seat of the big, gray car, Mr. Smith had Babba on one knee and Danny on the other, all buckled in with the same safety belt. Cisco and Poppy, one on each side, pressed up to him tightly as their own belts would allow. Boo, riding like a grown-up young woman up front with Mr. Monahan, wished for once that she could have been a middle child like Poppy, and not the eldest.

" . . . so we've got two weeks before I have to be back on the job in Pittsburgh," Mr. Smith explained. "You five and Granny can take care of each other once we're back there. Even in her wheelchair she's been cooking and trying to clean house. She'll be glad of the extra hands. But most important of all, I talked with Dr. Bachman, and he says that if I can guarantee that your mom'll stay in bed until the baby's due, and takes her medicine every day, she can leave the hospital tomorrow or Tuesday. So she'll stay at the Maldonados' house until September."

"Mrs. Maldonado promises she won't let Mom put a foot out of bed except to go to the bathroom," Boo put in.

"Good. The bossier she is, the better! And then Mom and the baby will fly home, and we'll all meet them at the Pittsburgh Airport." Mr. Smith gave Babba and Danny an extra hug. Boo and Cisco gave their father a quick look, but if he was worried about how he was going to pay the airfares and hospital bills and something to the Maldonados for expenses, he was too happy to show it.

"Now, you tell *me* the rest of what happened after Vulpo the Wolf Man and the Cookie Witch snatched the four Smiths," he said.

"That's right," Mr. Monahan said over his shoulder. "From where you left off: after they took Babba and Danny out burgling so they could scare Cisco and Poppy with the jail stories in case the kids caught on too soon."

Cisco and Babba, with interruptions from Poppy and Danny, poured out the story in a jumble of details, and Boo added her part. "Except," she finished, "it was the police who really did the rescue. As soon as Mr. Markle phoned and told them the license number, they knew where to go."

Mr. Monahan nodded. "Seems they've been keeping an eye on a 'fence,' one of the fellows who's been buying the Docketts' loot, and following anybody suspicious-looking who did business with him. This was back about six months ago and they didn't have any hard evidence to go on, so had to let it drop. But when they ran a check on the license number yesterday afternoon, the address popped right up on their computer. They didn't want to raid the place if they didn't have to—the kids might get hurt—so they set their little trap and hoped the Docketts would drive right into it."

Mr. Smith shook his head in wonder as he looked from one child to another. "Maybe the police did the rescuing, but I'm proud of the way all five of you kept your heads. Even Danny did his bit."

Danny opened his mouth wide, as if he meant to show just how loudly he had bellowed to help keep Ms. Cooperman from separating the children, but everyone in the car yelled "No!" just in time.

"The police say the other kids will go to relatives or foster homes back where they came from," Mr. Monahan said, "but it'll take a long time for 'em to catch up on their schooling. The Docketts'll stand trial here for kidnapping and grand theft, and Texas wants 'em too. That Sugar, their own kid, she could end up in Juvenile Hall."

J.D. and Peachie and the Baby Burglars, as one TV reporter had named them, had, it seemed, been doing four to six burglaries a week. The police had found in J.D.'s upstairs office the computer that he had used with a telephone connection to spy into travel agents' computers and find out when people in expensive neighborhoods were going to be traveling out of town. And when there were fancy electronic burglar alarms, he knew how to disconnect them. "A real copper-bottomed villain," Mr. Monahan said with a shake of his head.

Boo hesitated for a moment, and then asked a question that had been puzzling her since Saturday afternoon. "Mr. Monahan? Why'd you call Auntie Moss an old she-fraud?"

Mr. Monahan shrugged. "Because that's what she is. Oh, maybe she's still not running on all six cylinders, but she's not gaga, and yet she goes around making out as if she hasn't got two nickels to rub together. Don't you believe it. I happen to know that Calvin Moss had a little life insurance policy, and the year he died he was due to start collecting Social Security. So that old fraud not only has a little nest egg tucked away somewhere, but she must be getting something like five or six hundred dollars a month."

"But—but she *isn't,*" Boo protested. "All her mail used to come to our house, and she never got any checks, not ever."

Mr. Smith leaned forward with a frown. "That's right, Gus. And you know, I remember Frank Maldonado saying that while she was still living there next door after her husband died— this was while she was still off her rocker from missing him so much—she made a bonfire in the back yard and burned all his stuff, papers too, in a kind of funeral pyre, like he was some kind of king back in olden times. I'll bet you she never found out afterward that there was money she could put in for."

"Well, I'll be a—a ring-tailed monkey!" Mr. Monahan exclaimed. "It never occurred to me the old bat wouldn't know."

Boo's eyes shone. "You mean Auntie's going to be rich?"

"Rich?" Mr. Monahan guffawed. "Far from it. But she can afford to rent a room somewhere. And eat three meals a day." But then he frowned. "I wish I'd asked her about it a long time ago. Drat! I reckon that means I'm the one who ought to tell her now. Give her a hand with the paper-work, that kind of thing."

"Oh, I'm so glad!" Boo cried, but then she was suddenly doubtful. "I don't know. . . . She hates people telling her to do things and sign papers and all that."

"Still and all, I'll have to give it a try," Mr. Monahan said heavily as he turned in at the park-ing-lot entrance beside the Women's Hospital. He sighed. "And even if she gets back on track, I'll have to keep an eye on the old girl for a while. Make sure she doesn't let her battery run down again. Drat!"

Boo unfastened her safety belt and moved over to give his arm a hug. "Here now, here now!" Mr. Monahan said. "We're not parked yet. You'll have me bending somebody's fender. Anyhow, you forget about old Auntie for now. It's your mom we're here for."

"Just this once I'm going to bend the rules," Dr. Bachman said. "All of you children can go in with your father, but only to say hello and come straight back out. No excitement."

In the ward, Mrs. Smith stirred sleepily and smiled. "Oh, *there* you all are. What have you been up to since I keeled over?"

Boo looked at the others and grinned happily. "Nothing much," she said.

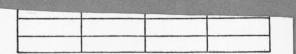